"Forgive Me, Tricia."

The hoarse cry in the night startled Tricia and she jolted awake. She sat up and stared at Jeremy. He was talking in his sleep again. She pushed off the chair and sat down on the mattress beside him.

"It's all right, Jeremy," Tricia crooned softly. "Everything is going to be all right, darling. I forgive you."

"I…I did not want to…to leave…you," he mumbled, still not opening his eyes.

Stretching out on the bed beside him, Tricia rested an arm over his chest, and blinking back tears, she tried to comfort him.

"I love you," she whispered in his ear. Rising on an elbow, she pressed her lips in a featherlight kiss on his temple.

Without warning Jeremy's eyes opened and he stared at her as if he had never seen her before. Tricia's heart beat a double-time rhythm. Had he heard her?

Dear Reader,

Welcome to another passionate month at Silhouette Desire where the menu is set with another fabulous title in our DYNASTIES: THE DANFORTHS series. Linda Conrad provides *The Laws of Passion* when Danforth heir Marc must clear his name or face the consequences. And here's a little something to whet your appetite—the second installment of Annette Broadrick's THE CRENSHAWS OF TEXAS. What's a man to do when he's *Caught in the Crossfire*— actually, when he's caught in bed with a senator's daughter? You'll have to wait and see....

Our mouthwatering MANTALK promotion continues with Maureen Child's *Lost in Sensation*. This story, entirely from the hero's point of view, will give you insight into a delectable male—what fun! Kristi Gold dishes up a tasty tidbit with *Daring the Dynamic Sheikh*, the concluding title in her series THE ROYAL WAGER. Rochelle Alers's series THE BLACKSTONES OF VIRGINIA is back with *Very Private Duty* and a hunk you can dig right into. And be sure to save room for the delightful treat that is Julie Hogan's *Business or Pleasure?*

Here's hoping that this month's Silhouette Desire selections will fulfill your craving for the best in sensual romance... and leave you hungry for more!

Happy devouring!

Melissa Jeglinski

Melissa Jeglinski
Senior Editor
Silhouette Desire

Please address questions and book requests to:
Silhouette Reader Service
U.S.: 3010 Walden Ave., P.O. Box 1325, Buffalo, NY 14269
Canadian: P.O. Box 609, Fort Erie, Ont. L2A 5X3

Very Private Duty

ROCHELLE ALERS

Silhouette®

Desire

Published by Silhouette Books

America's Publisher of Contemporary Romance

SILHOUETTE BOOKS

ISBN 0-373-76613-0

VERY PRIVATE DUTY

Copyright © 2004 by Rochelle Alers

This edition published by arrangement with Harlequin Books S.A.

® and TM are trademarks of Harlequin Books S.A., used under license.
Trademarks indicated with ® are registered in the United States Patent
and Trademark Office, the Canadian Trade Marks Office and in other
countries.

Visit Silhouette Books at www.eHarlequin.com

Printed in U.S.A.

Books by Rochelle Alers

Silhouette Desire

A Younger Man #1479
*The Long Hot Summer #1565
*Very Private Duty #1613

*The Blackstones of Virginia

ROCHELLE ALERS

is a native New Yorker who lives on Long Island. She admits to being a hopeless romantic, who is in love with life. Rochelle's hobbies include traveling, music, art and preparing gourmet dinners for friends and family members. A cofounder of Women Writers of Color, Rochelle was the first proud recipient of the Vivian Stephens Career Achievement Award for Excellence in Romance Novel Writing. You can contact her at P.O. Box 690, Freeport, NY 11520-0690, or roclers@aol.com.

Dedicated to:

Cheryl White—the first black woman jockey to ride on a U.S. commercial track at Thistledown Race Track in Cleveland, Ohio, on June 15, 1971.

Then the girls will dance and be happy, and the men, young and old, will rejoice. I will comfort them and turn their mourning into joy, their sorrow into gladness.

—*Jeremiah* 31:13

Prologue

"**I** never thought I'd say it, but I'm scared, Jeremy. I'm afraid of leaving you and Blackstone Farms." Her hushed tone trembled.

Jeremy Blackstone stared at Tricia. "There's nothing to be afraid of. New York and California are only three hours apart."

Tricia Parker was scheduled to fly from Virginia for New York to enroll in a premed program in less than twenty-four hours, leaving the protective, cloistered world of the horse farm behind.

"Let's get out of here, Jeremy."

He hesitated, then said, "Okay. Let's go." Jeremy

stood up, his arm curving protectively around her waist. They hadn't taken more than half a dozen steps when a familiar voice stopped them.

"Where are you going?"

Tricia turned and faced her grandfather. "We're going for a drive, Grandpa."

The lines in Augustus Parker's forehead deepened in frustration. "These people are here because of you, and you're walking out on them?"

"Grandpa, please don't start," she pleaded.

Gus gave Jeremy a level look. "I'd like to speak to my granddaughter for a few minutes. *Alone.*" He'd emphasized the last word.

Jeremy dropped his arm but not his gaze, holding the older man's direct stare. "Tricia, I'll wait for you outside."

Tricia watched Jeremy walk out of the main house's dining hall before her gaze returned to her grandfather's. "Grandpa, you don't understand—"

"What is there to understand, Tricia?" he said, interrupting her. "I have told you over and over not to get involved with the boss's son, because it's going to lead to no good."

She tilted her chin in a defiant gesture. "It's too late for that, because Jeremy and I *are* involved with each other. We plan to marry after we graduate from college."

"No, Tricia."

"Yes, Grandpa," she countered softly. "We're in love."

"Do you really think the son of the owner of one of the most profitable horse farms in the state of Virginia is going to marry the daughter of a woman who was a…" His words trailed off.

"A whore!" Tricia spat out the word. "Is that how you think of *me?*"

Lowering his head, Gus shook it slowly. "No, grandbaby girl. I know you're not a whore," he said in a quiet voice. "I just don't want you to get hurt."

She smiled. "Jeremy won't hurt me. He loves me too much for that." Rising on tiptoe, she kissed his cheek. "I've got to go. I'll see you later."

"Promise me you'll be careful."

Her smile widened. "I promise."

Tricia made her way out of the dining hall to the parking lot, coming face-to-face with the last person she wanted to see. She'd made certain to avoid him after he had once tried coming on to her. Russell Smith, three years her senior, was the head trainer's son. He was tall, dark and handsome, and he capitalized on his looks with every opportunity—especially with women.

"Leaving so soon, beautiful?"

"Yes, I am."

He smiled at her. "I wanted to give you a little something to celebrate your going off to college."

Tricia offered him a facetious smile. "Please give it to my grandfather for me."

Russell reached up, caught her chin and brushed a

gentle kiss over her lips. "I'll bring it by your house later."

Tricia resisted the urge to wipe the back of her hand over her mouth. "Suit yourself," she said through clenched teeth. Stepping around him she walked over to where Jeremy leaned against the bumper of his Jeep Wrangler.

Jeremy straightened and schooled his expression not to reveal what he was feeling—a slow-rising fury threatening to explode. "What's up with you and Smith?"

She stared up at him. "What are you talking about?"

His jaw hardened. "I'm talking about Russell Smith kissing you."

Tricia looped her arm through Jeremy's. "He was kissing me goodbye. I'm certain I'll get a few more goodbye kisses before I leave tomorrow." Rising on tiptoe, she kissed his earlobe. "You're the one I love, Jeremy," she said with feeling.

The tense lines in his face relaxed with her passionate confession. "Where do you want to go?"

"Surprise me," she whispered in his ear.

Jeremy helped her up onto the passenger seat, closed the door and rounded the SUV. He got in, turned the key in the ignition and drove out of the parking lot with a burst of speed. "Hang on, kid." Reaching up, Tricia grasped the roll bar as the Jeep literally ate up the road.

He maneuvered into a section of the farm referred

to as the north end and stopped under a copse of weeping willow trees next to a meandering stream. Using the headlights for illumination, he reached for a blanket in the space behind the seats and spread it on the ground. Then, he helped Tricia from the vehicle and settled her on the blanket, where they lay together holding hands.

Jeremy did not want her to leave Blackstone Farms any more than Tricia wanted to. He would follow her departure in two days. "You're so precious to me," he whispered against her parted lips.

Tricia's fingers were busy undoing the buttons on Jeremy's shirt while he deftly undid the hidden zipper down the back of her dress. "Don't talk," she whispered. "Just love me."

Mouths joined, they undressed quickly, leaving their discarded garments strewn over the blanket. Cradling her face between his palms, Jeremy eased her down to the blanket again as if she were a piece of fragile porcelain. Their own breathing drowned out the nocturnal sounds serenading the verdant valley nestled between the Blue Ridge and Shenandoah Mountain ranges.

Tricia inhaled the natural scent of Jeremy's skin mingling with his cologne. Her fingers tunneled through his rakishly long, inky-black wavy hair. She loved everything about him: his mysterious smoky-gray eyes, strong firm mouth and voice he rarely raised in anger.

His hairy chest grazed her breasts, her nipples hardening quickly. The motion heated her blood and ignited a fire that raced through her body and settled between her thighs. She knew without a doubt this coming together, the last one they would share for a long time, would not be the leisurely joining they'd experienced in the past.

Jeremy parted Tricia's legs with his knee and eased his sex into her hot, pulsing body. Both sighed as flesh melded with flesh, holding fast.

Tricia closed her eyes, savoring the hardness inside her. She was afraid to move because she did not want it to be over before it began. But her lover was not to be denied as he rolled his hips, sliding in and out, rocking back and forth. "Faster, Jeremy," she gasped, trembling as the little flutters grew stronger and stronger with each thrust.

Burying his face in the hollow between her neck and shoulder, Jeremy gritted his teeth, struggling not to release the straining passion in his loins. "No," he moaned as if in pain.

Her fingernails sank into the muscles in his firm buttocks. "Please."

He knew it was useless to fight the inevitable and quickened his motions until he did not know where he began and Tricia ended. They had become one in every sense of the word.

They climaxed at the same time, the sensations taking them higher than they had ever experienced together before, and released them in a shuddering ecstasy that seemed to go on and on. They lay motionless, their hearts beating in unison.

Jeremy wanted her again, but knew if he had seconds, then he'd want thirds and maybe fourths. It had always been that way with Tricia. She had become his drug of choice—one he did not want to ever give up.

Ten minutes after they'd washed away the evidence of their lovemaking in the shallow stream and put their clothes back on, they arrived at the two-bedroom bungalow where Tricia had grown up. Lights blazed from every window. The front door opened. Russell and Gus stepped out onto the porch and shook hands.

"Will I see you at breakfast?" Tricia's voice was barely a whisper.

Jeremy nodded. "Of course, sweetheart. I'll help you down."

She waited until he came around and swung her to the ground. "Good night, my love." Boldly, purposefully, she wound her arms around his neck, pulled his head down and kissed him.

Jeremy watched Tricia as she made her way up to the porch and walked into the house, Gus following. Grabbing the roll bar, he pulled himself up behind the wheel and released the brake.

"Hold up a minute, Blackstone."

His hand froze on the gearshift. He looked over at Russell. "What do you want?"

"I want to thank you."

"For what?"

Russell's lips twisted into a cynical smile. "For making it an easier ride in the saddle."

"What the hell are you talking about?"

"Tricia. You broke her in just right. I'm not one for virgins because I always find them too clingy. But Tricia's different. She doesn't mind sharing her goodies with the hired help as long as she can hold on to the boss's son." Doffing an imaginary hat, he walked back to his pickup truck parked alongside the bungalow.

Jeremy did not want to believe Russell, but he had seen him kiss Tricia. And what, he mused, was he doing at her place? A silent voice in his head screamed no because Tricia had said there was nothing between her and Russell...but a voice of reason said otherwise. However, there was only one way to uncover the truth. A minute later he stood on the porch, ringing the bell. Gus came to the door.

"I thought you and Tricia said good night."

"I'd like to talk to her again, sir."

Gus shook his head. "No, Jeremy. You've done enough damage."

"Pardon me, but just what is it I've done?"

The older man smiled, the expression softening his dark-brown face. "I like you, Jeremy, and I respect your father. But, I think it's best you leave my granddaughter alone."

"I can't do that, sir. Tricia and I—"

"There is no Tricia and you," Gus countered angrily. "Open your eyes, son. It's been Tricia and that young Smith fellow. He's planning to visit her in New York next month. He came over to give her this." Reaching into his slacks, he pulled a small velvet box from his pocket and opened it.

Jeremy stared at the delicate diamond heart. It was true. Russell hadn't lied. He was sleeping with Tricia and she was sleeping with both of them. He inclined his head. "You're right, Mr. Parker. Good night."

Jeremy threw underwear, T-shirts, socks and a pair of jeans into a suede duffel bag and zipped it. Moving like an automaton, he forced himself to put one foot in front of the other as he descended the staircase. Several feet from the front door he saw his father coming from the direction of the family room.

Sheldon stared at the bag in his hand. "Going somewhere?"

Jeremy swallowed to relieve the dryness in his constricted throat. "Yes, Pop. I'm going to spend a couple of days in Richmond. I'll be back Sunday night."

Sheldon's gaze narrowed in suspicion. "Are you all right, son?"

"Sure, Pop."

"Drive carefully."

Jeremy waved to his father as he opened the door, then closed it quietly behind him.

Tricia woke up early, showered and dressed in record time. She wanted to see Jeremy at the dining hall before he left for the track to watch the trainers put the horses through their exercise regimen. Her heart racing, she walked into the dining hall. Sheldon sat alone at a table. She headed for the owner of Blackstone Farms, a bright smile in place.

"Good morning, Sheldon."

His light-gray eyes bore into her as if she were a stranger. "Good morning, Tricia. Jeremy's not here."

She felt her heart stop, then start up again in a runaway rhythm. "Where is he?"

"He's staying in Richmond for a few days."

Tricia's hands closed into tight fists to conceal their trembling. "When did he leave?"

"Last night."

She closed her eyes for several seconds and when she opened them her gaze was steady. "Thank you."

He'd lied to her. Jeremy had promised to see her off, but it was apparent he had changed his mind. Perhaps, she thought, her grandfather was right. She should not have gotten involved with the boss's son.

She left the dining hall, head held high, fighting back tears. She promised herself she would never contact Jeremy Blackstone unless he contacted her first. And that was a promise she intended to keep.

One

Present Day

Eyes wide, her heart pumping rapidly and knees buckling slightly, Tricia Parker stared at the man sprawled on the Blackstones' leather sofa.

She could barely recognize Jeremy with all those bruises on his forehead, cheek and jaw. There was also a slight swelling over his right eye. Dressed in a white T-shirt and shorts, he was unshaved, his short black hair spiked, his left leg covered with a plaster cast from toe to knee, and the third and fourth fingers of his left hand were taped to a splint.

Only her nurses' training prevented Tricia from losing her composure when she saw the man to whom she had given her heart as an awestruck teenager. Each time she returned to Blackstone Farms a small part of her wanted to catch a glimpse of Sheldon Blackstone's youngest son, but it was as if their paths were destined not to cross again—until now.

"What happened to him?" Her voice was low, raspy, as if she had been screaming for hours.

Sheldon's light-gray eyes were fixed on Jeremy, who hadn't stirred since being placed on the sofa. "He had an accident—on the job," he added after a slight pause.

Tricia knew "on the job" for Jeremy was as a special agent with the Drug Enforcement Administration. He had graduated Stanford and instead of returning to Blackstone Farms he joined the U.S. Marine Corps. A month after he completed his military obligation he applied to the DEA as a special agent. She moved closer and placed a hand over his forehead. It was cool to the touch.

"How long has he been like this?"

"He was sedated before he was flown in from D.C.," Ryan Blackstone, Jeremy's older brother and the horse farm's resident veterinarian, said.

She withdrew her hand. "I'm talking about his injuries."

"Tomorrow will be two weeks," Sheldon said behind her. "He's going to need round-the-clock nursing care."

Tricia turned and stared at the imposing-looking owner of the most profitable African-American horse farm in the history of Virginia's horseracing. The years had been kind to Jeremy's father. Tall and solidly built, the middle-aged widower still had a full head of raven-black hair with a feathering of gray at the temples. He had extraordinary eyes: shimmering light gray in a golden-brown face.

"You want me to take care of him." Her question was a statement.

Sheldon inclined his head. "Yes."

"But, I'm only going to be here for a month." She had just begun her four-week vacation leave from her job as a registered nurse with a group of Baltimore pediatricians. "Don't you think it would be better to hire a permanent private-duty nurse?"

"I would if you weren't here. I'm certain Jeremy will respond much better to treatment with familiar faces around him. That's why I decided to bring him back to the farm."

A warning voice whispered in her head not to become involved with Jeremy again; however, she ignored it when she closed her eyes for several seconds. She wanted to decline Sheldon's request but couldn't. She had grown up on the farm, and tradition was that everyone looked after one another. Her gaze lingered on Sheldon before it shifted to Ryan.

"Okay."

Both men sighed.

Ryan closed the distance between them, cupped her elbow and led her into the dining room. His dark-gray eyes studied her intently. He was undeniably a Blackstone: height, complexion, raven hair, high cheek-bones, aquiline nose and mouth. As the older brother, he'd had most of the girls who had grown up on the horse farm fantasizing about marrying him, but not Tricia. Four years her senior, Ryan was too old and much too serious. Her choice had been Jeremy. They were the same age, carefree and at times very reckless.

Jeremy had earned the reputation of driving too fast, swearing and fighting too much, and he had been the one who had introduced her to a passion she had not experienced since.

"What am I dealing with, Ryan?"

"Broken ankle, dislocated fingers and a concussion. His ankle is held together with screws."

Tricia nodded. "Is there anything else I should know about your brother? Perhaps why he has been sedated, since it's not for pain?"

A sheepish grin softened the lines of tension around Ryan's mouth. "I could never fool you, Tricia. It's as if you have a sixth sense when it comes to Jeremy. The two of you must be bound by an invisible force that keeps you connected even though you've been separated for so many years."

A shiver snaked its way up her spine. There had been a time when she and Jeremy were able to complete each other's sentences. "You're wrong, Ryan," she said softly. "If that had been the case, then I would've known that something had happened to him. What aren't you telling me?"

"He has episodes—flashbacks of what happened to him and the other members of his team before he was rescued."

Her large dark eyes widened with this disclosure. It was obvious Jeremy was experiencing post-traumatic stress syndrome. "Was he tortured?"

Ryan shook his head. "I don't know. He was de-briefed, but as civilians we're not privy to that information."

"What are his meds?"

Ryan told her about the prescribed medication and dosage. "I'll make certain to give you the hospital's report. My brother is scheduled to see an orthopedist and a psychiatrist in a couple of days. I know this is your vacation, but I will make it up—"

"There's nothing to make up for," Tricia said, interrupting him. "Remember, I grew up here, and I've always thought of you and Jeremy as my brothers."

Ryan smiled. He wanted to tell Tricia that *he* had always thought of her as a younger sister, but not Jeremy. There was something about the assistant trainer's granddaughter that softened his brother, made him vulnerable. She would only stay a month, but perhaps it was long enough to help Jeremy adjust to coming home.

"He can't stay on the sofa," Tricia said. "He needs a bed and easy access to a bathroom."

"We plan to move him into his house in a few minutes. Things will go easier for you if he's under his own roof. A hospital bed has been set up in the family room. There's also a wheelchair, shower equipment and a pair of crutches. Sleeping arrangements will also be set up for you at his place, so I suggest you pick up what you'll need and then come back to Jeremy's place.''

Tricia nodded numbly as she walked out of the main house. Sheldon had houses built for his sons less than a quarter of a mile from the main house after they'd graduated from college.

Sleeping arrangements have been set up for you at Jeremy's place. Ryan's words echoed over and over as she drove back to the two-bedroom bungalow where she'd grown up with her grandparents.

She'd returned to Blackstone Farms to spend a month with Gus Parker, never believing she would have to share a house with the man she'd fallen in love with and continued to love even though she'd married another.

It had taken Dwight Lansing less than a year of marriage to realize his love and passion would never be reciprocated. A week before he and Tricia would have celebrated their first wedding anniversary, their marriage was annulled. She'd given her husband her body but never her heart. That she had given to Jeremy Blackstone to hold on to for eternity.

Jeremy surfaced from a drug-induced haze for the first time in hours. Long, thick black lashes framing a pair of deep-set, dove-gray eyes fluttered as he attempted to focus on the face looming over him.

The pain in his leg was forgotten as he stared up at the girl he hadn't seen in fourteen years. His eyes widened, moving slowly over her face and then lower. He stood corrected. Tricia Parker was not a girl, but a woman—all woman.

"Hi, Jeremy."

Her voice was soft and husky, the way he remembered it after they'd finished making love. She had been the one to do the talking when he couldn't, because making love had usually left him breathless and speechless.

The long, black curly hair that she'd worn in a braid was missing, in its place a short, cropped style that hugged her well-shaped head. Everything about her was ample: breasts, hips, round face, dark sparkling eyes and her mouth. Oh, how he'd loved kissing her mouth.

A white short-sleeved linen blouse and a pair of black slacks failed to camouflage or minimize her full figure. If her coloring had been a creamy magnolia instead of rich sable brown, she could have been the perfect model for baroque artist Peter Paul Rubens. Tricia was now the epitome of Rubenesque. It was as if she wore an invisible badge that silently announced: I Am Woman.

He closed his eyes, temporarily forgetting the deceitful woman hovering over him. "Where am I?"

"You're home."

"Home where?" He'd slurred the two words.

"In your house."

His eyes darkened like storm clouds. He'd waited fourteen, long agonizing years to reunite with Tricia so he could confront her about her infidelity. And now that that had become a reality, he knew he couldn't. Not when pain throbbed throughout his body.

"Get out of my house!"

Shaking her head, Tricia thrust her face close to his, feeling his moist breath sweep over her cheek. "I'm sorry, Jeremy, I can't do that."

Gray eyes glowing from his olive-brown face, like those of a savage predator, he bared his teeth. "I don't want you here."

Straightening, she rounded the bed, gently lifting his left foot to rest on two pillows. "It's not what you want but what you need. I'm going to be around for the next month, so you'd better get used to seeing me."

He went completely still. "A month?"

"Yes. I'm on vacation. Once it's over, I'm going back to Baltimore."

"I don't know if I can tolerate seeing you for a month."

"Stuff it, Jeremy," she retorted. "It's not as if I want to be bothered with you, either. But I promised your father that I'd look after you, and I'll do that until another nurse replaces me."

She neatly folded a lightweight blanket at the foot of the bed. What had been a family room was now a temporary bedroom. A tobacco-brown leather club chair with an ottoman was positioned several feet from the bed. The chair matched the daybed in a spacious alcove, which was now her temporary sleeping space. Sheldon had chosen the room because of an adjoining full bathroom with a freestanding shower.

Jeremy stared at Tricia. She did not look any older than when he last saw her, but she had changed, and it wasn't just her fuller figure or shorter hair. He'd lost count of the number of hours, days, months and years she'd continued to haunt him despite her duplicity. How could she profess to love him while she'd slept with another man at the same time? Had she told Russell Smith that she'd loved him, too?

"You didn't finish medical school." His question was a statement.

She straightened. "No, I didn't.

"What happened?"

"Nothing happened. I decided I wasn't cut out to be a doctor."

He lifted an eyebrow. "So, you became a nurse instead."

"Yes, Jeremy."

"Any specialty?"

She nodded, saying, "Pediatrics."

"You became a pediatric nurse instead of a pediatrician?"

Tricia wanted to scream at him that it had been his fault that she hadn't realized her dream to become a doctor. What neither knew when she'd left the farm to enter college was that she hadn't left alone. She was seven weeks' pregnant with Jeremy's baby, despite being on the Pill.

She had dropped out of college, given birth to a little girl and then lost her three months later, after they were run down by a speeding car. Her daughter died instantly, but Tricia spent weeks in the hospital with internal injuries.

The intoxicated driver, a celebrated matrimonial attorney to the rich and famous had the clout and resources to delay the case for years. Against her attorney's advice, Tricia settled out of court for less than she would've received if the case had gone to trial. At that time in her life she had been too depressed to relive the ordeal in a lengthy trial.

She did not blame the drunk driver for killing her baby. Tricia blamed Jeremy. And if he hadn't deserted her she could've returned to the farm to live. He had deserted her and their infant daughter.

She married her attorney, but only after he insisted they sign a prenuptial agreement. Dwight Lansing claimed he wanted to marry her because he loved her and not for her money.

"And you became a DEA agent instead of coming back to run the horse farm," she retorted sharply.

"We're not talking about me, Tricia."

"And I don't intend to talk about *me*, Jeremy. For the next month you and I are patient and nurse and nothing else."

Despite the pain in his head surpassing the one in

his leg, he affected a snappy salute with his uninjured hand. "Yes, ma'am!"

She managed to hide a smile as she made her way to the windows and closed the vertical blinds, shutting out some of the bright sunlight pouring into the room. "Someone will deliver lunch in a few minutes. After that I'm going to help you get out of bed, even if it's just for half an hour."

"I'm not ready to get out of bed."

"Your doctor wants you out of bed."

"He's not here, so what he says doesn't mean spit!"

Tricia struggled to control her temper. As a pediatric nurse she had encountered children with a variety of illnesses and deformities, but invariably she was always able to coax a smile from them. Jeremy wasn't a child, but a thirty-two-year-old man who had chosen a career that put him at risk every day of his life. He was alive, and for that he should've been grateful, not angry and resentful.

"You will follow my directives." Her voice was soft yet threatening. "You need me to feed you and assist you with your personal hygiene." She knew he wouldn't be able to feed himself easily because he was left-handed. "Growl at me one more time and I'll take my time helping you to the bathroom. Lying in one's own waste is not the most pleasant experience."

Jeremy gave Tricia a long, penetrating look. How had she known? He and the three surviving members from a DEA Black Op team of six had hidden out in a swamp in the Peruvian jungle for forty-eight hours before they were rescued. Not only had they lain in their own waste but they'd been bitten repeatedly by insects. His team leader had come down with a fever and died within an hour of being airlifted to safety.

He had no more fight left in him—at least not today. His head felt as if it was exploding. He wanted to tell Tricia that he knew how to use a pair of crutches and hobble, albeit slowly, to the bathroom, but decided not to antagonize her further.

"All right," he said, deciding to concede. "You win, Tricia." And she would remain the winner, but only until his pain eased. "I'll get out of bed." Closing his eyes, he clenched his teeth.

"Are you in pain?"

He squinted. "My head."

"I'll take your vitals, then I'll give you something to take the edge off." Ryan had left a blood pressure kit and a digital thermometer for her use.

Jeremy suffered Tricia's gentle touch and the hauntingly familiar scent of her body as she took his temperature and blood pressure. She gave him a pill and a glass of water, watching closely as he placed it on his tongue. She recorded the readings on a pad and the time she had given him the painkiller.

"Drink all of the water."

He complied, handing her the empty glass. Their gazes met and fused. "Thank you," he mumbled reluctantly.

Her passive expression did not change. "You're welcome."

She was there, and then she was gone, taking her warmth and scent with her. And it had been her smell that, years ago, had drawn Jeremy to Tricia. She always wore perfume when the other girls on the farm smelled of hay and horses.

Sighing heavily, he closed his eyes. His father and brother complained they did not see him enough. And whenever he did return home it was never for more than a few days. There had been a time when Blackstone Farms was his whole world but after joining the DEA, the war on drugs had become his life. He always came back to reconnect with his family, but refused to stay.

He lay in the dimly lit room listening to the sound of his own heart beating. He hadn't realized he had fallen asleep until he felt the soft touch on his arm and a familiar voice calling his name.

"Wake up, Jeremy. It's time to eat."

Seeing Tricia again, inhaling her familiar feminine scent reminded him of what he'd been denying for nearly half his life. He hadn't returned to Blackstone Farms after graduating from college because of the memories of a young woman to whom he had pledged his future. He had loved her unconditionally while she had deceived him with another man.

Whenever he visited the farm a part of him had hoped to see Tricia, but they never connected—until now. And whenever he asked her grandparents about her, their response was always, "She's doing just fine in the big city."

He shifted on the bed, groaning softly as pain shot through his ankle. Compressing his lips, he managed to somehow find a more comfortable position as Tricia adjusted the bed's tray table.

The moment she uncovered a plate he closed his eyes. "I want some real food."

She placed a cloth napkin over his chest. "This is real food."

He opened his eyes, his expression thunderous. "Broth, applesauce and weak-ass tea!"

She picked up a soup spoon. "You've been on a light diet. It's going to take time before you'll be able to tolerate solids." He clamped his jaw tight once she put the spoon to his mouth. "Open!"

He shook his head, chiding himself for the action. Each time he moved, intense pain tightened like a vise on his head. "No," he hissed between clenched teeth.

Tricia bit down on her lower lip in frustration and stared at the stubborn set of his jaw. Broken, battered and bruised he still had the power to make her heart race. "You're going to have to eat or you'll be too weak to get out of bed."

He glared at her. "Get me some food, Tricia. Now!"

She glared back in what she knew would become a standoff, a battle of wills. "I'm certain I warned you about raising your voice to me. Eat the broth and applesauce and I'll call the dining hall to have them send something else.''

"What?''

''You can have either Jell-O or soft scrambled eggs.''

''How about steak and eggs?''

''Not yet, hotshot. Once you're up and moving around I'll put in an order for steak and eggs. And if you actually cooperate, then you can have pancakes.'' Everyone at Blackstone Farms knew how much Jeremy loved the chef's pancakes. He opened his mouth and she fed him the soup.

''Is he giving you a hard time?'' asked a familiar voice.

Tricia shifted slightly and stared over her shoulder at Ryan. He had entered the room without making a sound. ''No.''

Jeremy swallowed the bland liquid. ''She's giving me a hard time. This stuff is as bad as castor oil.''

Ryan pushed aside the ottoman as he sat on the roomy leather chair. He smiled and attractive lines fanned out around his eyes. He ran his left hand over his cropped hair, and a shaft of light coming through the blinds glinted off the band on his finger. He'd married the resident schoolteacher last summer, and now he and Kelly awaited the birth of their first child together. Ryan had a five-year-old son, Sean, from a prior marriage.

''It can't be that bad, little brother.''

Jeremy grimaced. ''Worse.''

Ryan raised his eyebrows. "You better follow your nurse's orders and get your butt out of that bed as soon as possible."

Jeremy swallowed two more spoonfuls. "Why?"

"Kelly woke up this morning with contractions. They're not that strong, about twenty minutes apart, but there's a good chance she'll have the baby either today or tomorrow, and I know when I bring your niece home you don't want her to see her uncle flat on his back."

Jeremy managed a smile, but it looked more like a grimace. "I thought Kelly wasn't due until the end of the month." It was now the second week in July.

"She's farther along than was first predicted. Babies are smarter than we are. They know exactly when to make their grand entrance. Don't you agree, Tricia?"

She nodded. The words she wanted to say were locked in her constricted throat. She wanted to tell Ryan that she had given Sheldon Blackstone his first granddaughter. A little girl she'd named Juliet to honor the memory of Jeremy's mother Julia—a little girl who'd been undeniably a Blackstone.

Tricia wanted to run out of the room, leaving the brothers to discuss the upcoming birth of Kelly's daughter. She drew a deep breath, forbidding herself to cry. Not in front of Jeremy.

"Ryan, could you please finish feeding your brother? I'd like to look in on my grandfather for a few minutes.'' She had to escape before she broke down.

She'd left Gus earlier that morning after Sheldon had come to the bungalow asking her help in caring for Jeremy. The look on the older man's face spoke volumes. It was fear. There was no doubt he was afraid she would become involved with Jeremy again; she wanted to reassure her grandfather that would not happen a second time.

Ryan stood up, exchanging seats with Tricia. ''Take your time with Gus. If I have to leave, then I'll call my father to come and sit.''

She took a quick glance at her patient. His chest rose and fell in a measured rhythm. He had fallen asleep. Her gaze softened as she studied his face in repose. Juliet had been a miniature, feminine version of her father.

A shudder shook her as the import of what had become a reality for three short months struck her. She and Jeremy had been parents of a little girl who had righted all of the wrongs—a baby she loved with all of her heart.

Tricia found Gus sitting on the porch, rocking in his favorite chair, eyes closed. She stood on the lower step and stared at her grandfather. Tall and slender, there wasn't an extra ounce of flesh on his spare frame and for the first time she saw him as an old man. He had celebrated his seventy-seventh birthday that spring. She mounted the steps slowly, and he opened his eyes to stare up at her.

"How is he?"

"*He* does have a name, Grandpa."

"Okay. How is Jeremy?"

"He's going to live." Smiling, she pulled over a rattan chair, facing her grandfather.

Gus returned her smile. The gesture took years off his face. "That's good."

"Is it, Grandpa?"

His smile vanished. "I've always liked Jeremy."

"You liked him, but not for me."

"I was trying to protect you, Tricia."

"Protect me from what or whom?" she asked, leaning forward on the cushioned seat.

"I just didn't want you to end up like your mother."

Gus had attempted to protect Tricia, but she did end up like her mother. She'd gotten pregnant and had become a teenage mother. But unlike Patricia, she had not abandoned her baby.

"She could've aborted me, but she didn't."

"I'm thankful she didn't, because who else would I have in my old age."

"You're not old, Grandpa."

Gus sucked his teeth. "I'm old and you know it. And what bothers me is that I've become an old fool. If I hadn't interfered with you and Jeremy, I know the two of you would've married years ago. And there's no doubt I would've had at least two or three great-grandchildren by now.''

Tricia stared at the climbing roses on the trellis attached to the side of the house. The roses had been her grandmother's pride and joy. ''What's done is done.''

Gus stared at his granddaughter's solemn expression. ''You still love him, don't you?''

Turning her head, she looked directly at him. ''Why would you ask me that?''

''Because I need *you* to tell me the truth, Tricia. When you called your grandmamma and me to tell us you were marrying that lawyer fellow neither of us could believe it because you never mentioned his name whenever you called us. And when we came up to New York to meet him, the first thing Olga said to me was that you didn't love him. That's why we never told anyone at the farm that you'd married. Olga knew it wasn't going to last. But what hurt most was that a stranger had to tell us that you'd had our great-granddaughter.''

''I told you why I did not want to tell you. At that point in my life I wasn't equipped to listen to you preach about how I'd become my mother. What you failed and still fail to see is that I am who I am. I may look like my mother, but that's where the similarity ends. Yes, I had a baby, but I did not desert my daughter.

''Even though I was a full-time student, I got a job, saved my money, passed all my courses and made arrangements for child care before Juliet was born. I managed to hold everything together until the accident. Then, I didn't care whether I lived or died. I'd lost my baby, and then Grandmamma died two years later. I carried a lot of guilt, Grandpa, because I kept telling myself that if I'd come back to the farm when I realized I was pregnant, my baby wouldn't have died.''

Leaning back on the rocker, Gus sighed. ''But you didn't come back, because you didn't want to hear me say 'I told you so.'''

''That wasn't the only thing, Grandpa. I wanted to see if I could make it on my own,'' she half lied. What she had not wanted to do was use her child as a pawn to get Jeremy to come back to her.

Gus shook his head. ''Olga, God rest her soul, always told me that I was better with horses than human beings.''

Tricia smiled. ''That's because horses don't talk back.''

''Amen, grandbaby girl.'' He waved a gnarled hand. ''Don't you think it's time you get back to your young man?''

''He's my *patient*, Grandpa, not my young man.'' She stood up. ''Did you eat lunch?'' Even though her grandfather had retired at seventy-five he continued to live on the horse farm and rent the bungalow. The cost of meals was included in his monthly rental.

Gus patted his flat belly over a pair of well-washed denim overalls. ''I ate a big breakfast.''

Leaning over, she kissed his cheek. "Don't forget to eat dinner."

"I won't." He waved his hand again. "Go on!"

Tricia drove the short distance back to Jeremy's house. She was surprised to find Sheldon instead of Ryan sitting in the club chair. He stood up.

"I told Ryan I'd sit with him until you got back."

"I'll take over now."

"Ryan also told me that you haven't eaten, so I'll have your lunch delivered."

"Thank you."

Sheldon walked out, and Tricia sat down on the chair he'd vacated, watching the man she had fallen in love with so many years ago sleep.

Two

Jeremy woke up, his glazed gaze fixed on the ceiling. "Jump! Jump now, dammit!"

Tricia sat up in a jerky motion like a marionette on a string, her heart pounding wildly in her chest. She shot up from the chair and raced over to the bed. Jeremy's right arm flailed wildly, his elbow striking her shoulder and knocking her backward. Recovering quickly, she lay over his chest, holding his arms at his sides.

"Jeremy, Jeremy," she said, crooning his name over and over. "It's all right. You're safe, darling." The endearment had slipped out unbidden.

He heard the voice, felt the comforting weight of a soft body and inhaled the familiar feminine fragrance that made him think of other times in his life when two motherless youngsters found comfort in each other's embraces. The frightening images faded as quickly as they had come and Jeremy buried his face in the curly hair grazing his jaw.

"Tricia?"

"Go back to sleep."

"I...I...love..." His words trailed off.

Tricia went completely still. Who was he talking about? Was there a woman who had captured Jeremy's heart the way she'd done? He had come back to Blackstone Farms, but did he have a fiancée somewhere who awaited his return?

Her fingertips massaged his temples in a circular motion. "It's all right, Jeremy. Everything's going to be all right."

"You won't leave me?"

Tricia shook her head before she realized Jeremy couldn't see her. Why did he sound so helpless, vulnerable? "No, Jeremy, I won't leave you."

"Please, get into bed with me."

"I can't."

"Why not? You used to sleep with me."

"That was before and this is now. I'm your nurse and you're my patient."

He gritted his teeth, slowly letting out his breath. He'd gripped her shoulder with his injured fingers. "Please stay with me until I go back to sleep."

Sleeping with a patient was unprofessional and unethical. The difference in having Jeremy Blackstone as a patient was that at one time she *had* slept with him.

Easing out of his embrace, she lowered the railing and lay down on his right side. All the memories of her sharing a bed with him came rushing back as if it were yesterday instead of fourteen years before. She lay motionless as everything about her first lover enveloped her in a longing that she had forgotten.

"Tricia?"

She smiled. Why did he always make her name sound like a caress? "Yes, Jeremy."

"Thank you."

It was the second time he'd thanked her. "You're welcome."

Waiting until she heard the soft snores indicating Jeremy had gone back to sleep, Tricia slipped off the bed. *It's not going to work.* The five words slapped at her. How was she going to share a bedroom, touch her first lover's body and not lose it? She'd had fourteen years to tell herself that she hated Jeremy for deserting her, but just coming face-to-face with him had made a liar of her.

She'd done the very thing her grandfather had warned her against. She had given Jeremy her heart, her innocence and her love, for eternity.

Making her way over to the daybed, she lay down, resting her head on folded arms. Now she knew why Sheldon wanted a private-duty nurse for Jeremy. They did not want him alone during his flashback episodes. The expression on his face had been one of pure terror, and again she wondered if he had been held prisoner or tortured during his captivity.

The attending doctor at the military hospital had written referrals for Jeremy to see an orthopedist and a psychiatrist, and there was no doubt his body would heal before his mind did.

She remembered what Sheldon had said about Jeremy responding positively to treatment if he was in familiar surroundings. A knowing smile crinkled her eyes. She and Jeremy could not turn back the clock, but she could attempt to recapture some of the magic from their childhood.

Jeremy woke up for the first time, since he'd regained consciousness in the Washington, D.C., hospital, without the blinding pain in his head. He'd lost track of time but knew he was home when he heard the soothing strains of violins playing Mozart's "Serenade in G Major." It had been a long time since he'd heard that selection.

Lifting his head off the pillows cradling his shoulders, he sniffed the air and smiled. He could smell brewing coffee. What he'd liked most about his South American missions had been the coffee. Colombian and Brazilian coffees were some of the best blends in the world. However, he couldn't lie in bed savoring the smell of coffee or listening to music, because he had to use the bathroom. There was one problem: he couldn't get out of the bed without help.

"Hello," he called out.

Seconds later Tricia appeared. She looked different from before. She'd exchanged her blouse and slacks for a sunny-yellow sundress with a squared neckline that skimmed her lush body. Other than her short hair, it had been the changes to her body that had caught his immediate attention. When he'd left Tricia, her body hadn't claimed the womanly curves she now flaunted shamelessly. The pressure in the lower portion of his body increased, and Jeremy knew it had nothing to do with his need to relieve himself.

"Hi."

She flashed a shy smile, her expression reminiscent of one she'd offered him what now seemed so long ago. "Good morning, Jeremy." She looked at her watch. "It's six-twenty."

He scratched his cheek with his right hand at the same time his stomach grumbled. He had been asleep for more than fifteen hours. "I need to use the bathroom."

Nodding, Tricia picked up a pair of crutches. She moved over to the bed, lowered a side rail and handed him the crutches. He took them with his uninjured hand while she gently swung his legs over the side of the mattress.

"Put your left arm around my neck and pull yourself up with your right hand, using the crutches for support."

He completed the task without difficulty, but had to anchor the thumb and forefinger of his left hand over the rubber-covered handgrip. It would be some time before he'd be able to make a fist with that hand.

"Steady, hotshot," Tricia cautioned softly.

Jeremy took several halting steps before he regained his balance. "I've got it."

She looked up at him, her dark gaze fusing with his. "Do you need me to help you?"

His gaze grew wider as he took in everything about her in one sweeping glance. They had lost so much. It had taken them a long time to reunite, but now they were different people. It was as if they'd become polite strangers.

"No, thank you. I believe I have everything under control."

Lowering her gaze, she nodded. "Call me when you're finished." He nodded and hobbled slowly to the bathroom.

Tricia stripped the bed and remade it with clean linens while she waited for Jeremy to call her. She'd gotten up earlier that morning and had taken a tour of his home. It was an exact replica of the one where he'd grown up, except on a smaller scale. The three-bedroom house was constructed with enough room for a family of four to live comfortably without bumping into one another. She'd stood in the middle of the master bedroom suite, wondering if she had come back once her pregnancy was confirmed whether she would have slept beside Jeremy in the king-size wrought-iron bed or sat in the sitting room nursing their daughter.

She'd dismissed those thoughts as soon as they'd entered her head because she could not afford to think of what would've been. And the reality of the present was that she would give Jeremy the next four weeks of her life. No more than that.

The last disc on the CD player ended, filling the space with silence. She glanced at her watch. Jeremy had been in the bathroom for more than a quarter of an hour.

Tricia made her way to the bathroom and knocked on the door. "Jeremy?"

"Come in." His voice was muffled.

She pushed open the door and found him sitting on a stool in front of a generous serpentine-marble washbasin, peering into a marble-rimmed oval mirror anchored to a length of wall mirrors. The mirrors made the space appear twice its size. His jaw was covered with shaving cream as he attempted to shave himself with his right hand. The day before he hadn't wanted to get out of bed, and now he was attempting to groom himself.

Closing the distance between them, she took the razor from his grasp. "Why didn't you call me?"

Jeremy's head came up, and he saw the frown marring Tricia's smooth forehead. "I wanted to see if I could shave myself. I did manage to brush my teeth."

"Brushing your teeth is safer than shaving. What if you'd cut yourself?"

He lifted a thick, curving black eyebrow. "If I cut my throat, then that would let you off the hook."

Her frown deepened. "What are you talking about?"

"I'd bleed to death, then you wouldn't have to take care of me."

Her fingers tightened on the handle of razor. "Did I say I didn't want to take care of you?"

"I know you don't want to be here with me. You're only doing it because my father asked you."

Tricia crossed her arms under her breasts. "Let's clear the air about something. I'm here because you're my patient, so don't read more into our association than that."

He angled his head, studying her gaze for a hint of guile. "Okay, Tricia, if that's what you want."

"It is," she said quickly.

Shifting, she stood directly in front of him. Cradling his chin in her hand, she lifted his face. Dots of blood showed through the layer of cream. "You've already cut yourself." Turning on the hot water faucet, she rinsed the blade, then began scraping away the wiry black whiskers. His face was leaner, cheekbones more pronounced. He'd lost weight.

Jeremy was hard-pressed not to laugh. Tricia's breasts were level with his gaze. Mesmerized, he watched the gentle swell of dark brown flesh rise and fall above the revealing décolletage.

"Did you bring any uniforms with you?"

Her hand halted under his chin. "No. Why?"

A knowing smile crinkled the network of lines around his eyes—lines that were the result of squinting in the tropical sun. "I'm getting quite an eyeful of certain part of your anatomy with you in that dress."

Her gaze lowered as heat suffused her cheeks. She moved the blade closer to his brown throat. "Don't you know it's risky to mess with a woman who's holding a sharp razor at your throat?"

His eyes darkened until they appeared as black as his pupils. "No more risky than my falling in love with you fourteen years ago."

Her hand trembled slightly. "No, Jeremy," she whispered.

Vertical lines appeared between his eyes. "No! No *what?*"

"Let's not talk about the past."

Reaching up, he wrested the razor from her fingers. "Yes, Tricia, let's talk about it. Let's clear the air so we can move on."

She flinched at the tone of his voice. "I've moved on."

"Well, I haven't."

"Whose problem is that?"

"It's our problem, Tricia." His voice was noticeably softer. "Every time I came back I'd ask your grandfather how you were doing, and he always had a pat answer. 'Tricia's doing well,' or 'she loves living in New York.' You loved New York so well that you moved to Baltimore?"

She nodded. "I moved to Baltimore after my divorce."

He went completely still. Her grandfather never mentioned her marrying. His chest rose and fell as his pulse raced uncontrollably. "You were married?"

"Yes."

Jeremy sucked in a lungful of breath, held it as long as he could before letting it out, feeling himself relaxing, albeit slowly. When he'd least expected it, memories of what they'd shared crept under the barrier he'd erected to keep other women out of his life and his bed. Each nameless face had become Tricia's. Their voices her voice. After a while he gave up altogether and succumbed to prolonged periods of celibacy.

"How long were you married?"

Tricia retrieved the razor and resumed the task of scraping away the coarse black whiskers from his chin and jaw. "Not long." Her voice was as neutral as her touch.

"How long is not long?"

Smoothly they'd slipped back into the comfortable familiarity of confiding in each other, because they'd been friends longer than they'd been lovers.

"It was over before we celebrated our first anniversary."

"What happened?"

"We were not compatible."

"Didn't you know that before you married him?" She nodded. "Why did you marry him, anyway?"

"I was very vulnerable at the time."

"Which meant he took advantage of you."

She shook her head. "No, Jeremy, he did not take advantage of me. I knew what I was doing. It was a period in my life when I did not want to be alone." She put the razor in the basin.

Reaching for a damp towel on the nearby countertop, Jeremy wiped away dots of shaving cream. "Why didn't you come back to live with your grandfather if you didn't want to be alone?"

Tricia took the towel from his loose grip and dabbed at the nicks. "I couldn't come back—at least not to stay."

He curved his right arm around her waist, pulling her closer. For several moments they fed on each other, offering strength and comfort. Resting her chin on the top of his head, Tricia closed her eyes. It was so easy to slip back in time—a time when they could talk about any and everything, a time when they weren't afraid to tell the other their most heartfelt secrets and a time when they were young, fearless and hopelessly in love with life and each other.

"What about now, Tricia? Are you ready to stay?"

She curbed an urge to kiss his hair as she'd once done. The man embracing her may sound the same, but she knew he was not the same. The short spiky black hair and pierced earlobes belonged to a stranger, someone she recognized but no longer knew.

"No," she said after a pregnant pause.

"Why not?"

"Because I have a life in Baltimore."

He raised his head and his gray gaze searched her face, looking for a remnant of the girl he had grown up with—the one who'd captured his heart with her vulnerability, the one he'd protected from the other children who repeated gossip they'd heard from their parents about her mother.

He flashed a wry smile. "Is there someone waiting for you in Baltimore?"

Tricia thought of one of the doctors in the group where she worked. She and Wade had dated casually over the past two months, although he'd expressed a desire for it to become more than casual.

Easing out of his loose embrace, Tricia shook her head. "No," she answered truthfully.

"Then there is a distinct possibility that you could come back to Blackstone Farms to work?"

"And do what?"

"Blackstone Farms Day School will officially operate as a private school this September. Kelly has interviewed and hired teachers for prekindergarten through sixth grade. All of the farm children will attend the school along with additional children from several neighboring farms. I believe there is still an opening for a school nurse."

A lump settled in Tricia's throat, making swallowing difficult. What Jeremy was offering was a perfect solution for her. She could be close to her grandfather and still pursue her career. It had taken Gus more than a decade to apologize in his own way without actually saying he was sorry, but he finally had.

If her grandfather hadn't interfered, she would've married Jeremy and Gus would have had a beautiful great-grandchild to spoil or bounce on his knee. But Tricia was a realist and she knew she could not go back in time to right past wrongs. She'd made a new life for herself and there was no place in her life for Jeremy. She could not trust him not to desert her again.

If she had to take care of her grandfather, once he was no longer able to care for himself, then she would take him to Baltimore with her. The row house she'd purchased in the fashionable suburban community had three bedrooms—more than enough room for her and Gus.

"I'm certain becoming a school nurse would be a new and wonderful experience for me, but I like where I live and I love what I do."

Angling his head again, Jeremy stared up at her through half-closed eyes. She liked where she lived and loved her career, while he felt as if he were swimming through a haze of doubt and uncertainty. His injuries and the possibility that he might never be medically cleared to participate in future undercover missions made Jeremy consider his future.

He had wasted too many years running away when he should've stayed and confronted Tricia about Russell Smith. He'd realized that the afternoon he lay in bed in a Richmond hotel, staring at the clock, aware that she was on a jet flying to New York.

He had come back over the years to see his father, brother, nephew and sister-in-law, but he also had come back to see Tricia—to ask her why.

"Are you ready for your shower?"

Tricia's soft voice broke into his thoughts. "I will be, after you answer one question for me."

"What's that?"

"Why did you ever sleep with Russell Smith?"

Three

——

Tricia blinked once, as if coming out of a trance, not certain whether she had heard Jeremy correctly. Had he asked her if she had slept with Russell Smith? It had been years since she had given the man a passing thought, and that was to tell her grandfather she did not want Russell's graduation gift. She'd told Gus to return it sight unseen.

"Do you actually expect me to answer that?" she retorted with cold sarcasm.

Jeremy nodded. "I'd like you to."

She stared wordlessly at him for several seconds. "This is not about what you'd like, Jeremy." Tricia was surprised her voice was so calm when her heart was pounding an erratic rhythm. "If you'd asked me that question fourteen years ago I would've given you an answer. But there has been too much time between us. I've changed, while it's apparent you haven't. I'm your nurse, not your girlfriend. As long as you remember that, we will get along famously.''

Jeremy's luminous eyes widened as he glared at her. ''You weren't my girlfriend, Tricia. You were my fiancée. I'd offered to give you a ring, but it was you who wanted to wait until after we'd graduated from college. If you had been wearing my ring, then that would've kept the other boys from following you around.''

''The only one who followed me was you, Jeremy. And it wasn't until I stood still long enough that you caught me.''

His black lashes concealed his gaze from hers as he stared at the thick plaster cast protecting his shattered ankle. ''Did you regret it?''

''No.'' His head came up and she met his direct stare. ''I didn't regret it, because at that time I was ready to give up my virginity. And, why not to the boss's son?''

If Tricia had sought to wound Jeremy as much as he had her, then she knew she succeeded when she saw his expression. His black eyebrows were drawn together in an agonized expression.

Jeremy swallowed back curses—raw, ugly, violent, crude ones he hadn't spewed in years—curses that used to bring tears to his mother's eyes and a threat to wash his mouth out with soap. He had continued to swear until her threats became a reality. Despite detesting the taste of lye soap he had still cursed, but tried never to do it in her presence.

Tricia did not have to tell him if she'd slept with Russell, because her response validated Russell's claim: *She doesn't mind sharing her goodies with the hired help as long as she can hold on to the boss's son.*

He wasn't angry with Tricia but himself, because he had opened a wound he had permitted to heal, a wound with a noticeable scar. Now he was bleeding again. No, he told himself. What he'd had with Tricia was over, never to be resurrected.

With his jaw clenched, he captured and held Tricia's dark, slanting eyes. "You're right about our roles as nurse and patient. I'll make certain never to forget that as long as you're here. Now, if you don't mind I'm ready to take my shower."

The short, curling hair on the nape of Tricia's neck stood up. It wasn't what Jeremy had said but how he'd said it that held a silken thread of warning.

Nodding, she relieved him of the T-shirt. Her mouth went dry as she stared at a broad chest covered with thick black hair. Jeremy's upper body was magnificent: defined pectorals, massive biceps and flat abs. Despite his broken ankle, he was in peak condition.

She kept her expression and touch neutral as she relieved him of his shorts, underwear and covered his left leg and foot with the plastic cast sheath, tight-

ening the Velcro band around his thigh. Jeremy hobbled on crutches to the circular shower and sat down
on a stool under a ten-inch showerhead that was cen-
trally positioned overhead. She handed him a plastic
bottle filled with liquid soap, a cloth, and removed an
auxiliary hand shower from the wall.

She picked up the crutches. "Do you want me to
turn on the water?" The faucets were within arm's
reach.

Jeremy shook his head. "No, thank you. I'll manage."

Tricia met his impassive gaze. "Call me when
you're finished." Not waiting for his reply, she
walked out of the bathroom.

She stood next to the hospital bed and sucked in a
lungful of air. It had taken every ounce of her will-
power not to glance below his waist. She had concentrated on the bruises dotting his body instead.

She had told herself that she was a nurse and as
one she had seen countless nude men in various
stages of arousal during her nursing school training.
Some thought they could shock her whenever they
summoned her to their beds to look at what they'd
considered their masculine prowess, but what they did
not know was that none of them would ever affect
her the way her first lover had done. It wasn't until
after she'd married Dwight that she realized she was
a one-man woman. That man was Jeremiah Baruch
Blackstone. And she had not wanted to look at her
first lover to see whether she still turned him on, be-

cause she knew she wasn't as immune to him as she wanted to be.

And if the truth be told, she still wanted him in her bed. She had never stopped wanting him in her bed.

As directed, Jeremy called out to Tricia that he had finished his shower. She reentered the bathroom, and the lingering steam settled around her, dampening her face and hair. His stare was fixed on her grim expression as she dried his wet body with a thirsty terry cloth towel. She removed the plastic covering from his leg, checking for moisture seepage. Twenty minutes later he sat at a table on the porch, wearing a T-shirt and shorts, his left foot propped up on a low stool.

He watched Tricia like a hawk as she set a table with china and silver. She had only put out one serving. "Aren't you going to eat?"

Her head came up. "I'll eat later."

"I'd like you to eat *now*."

Tricia held his gaze. "If you want me to eat with you, why not ask me to…politely."

A slight smile tugged at the corners of his mouth. "I want you to take *all* of your meals with me."

Tricia had forgotten that Jeremy never ate alone after his mother's untimely death. Even though the farm had a resident chef, Julia Blackstone had always cooked dinner. That had been her time to bond with her husband and sons.

She nodded. "I'll get another place setting."

He sat motionless, staring out at the lushness of the property surrounding his house. Massive oak trees with sweeping branches provided a canopy of shade for the manicured lawn that resembled an undulating green carpet.

A knowing smile softened his mouth and crinkled the skin around his eyes. Blackstone Farms was beautiful, almost as beautiful as the primordial jungles of South America.

He closed his eyes and thought about the men on his team, men who had lived together for so long they knew the others' thoughts, men who, over the course of several years, had become as close as brothers. The six of them had trained together in Quantico, Virginia, honing their physical and mental skills. He'd become an expert in firearms, fitness and defensive tactics, as well as defensive driving training. His olive coloring and fluency in Spanish and additional intelligence training courses made him a natural candidate for undercover missions in Latin America.

He opened his eyes, reached up with his uninjured hand and ran his fingers through his short damp hair. He had been debriefed by his superiors and informed that the probability of his returning to undercover work was questionable. The orthopedist's prognosis stated that although he would walk again without too much difficulty, the damage to his ankle would never withstand the rigors of duty in the field.

All thoughts of his future with the Drug Enforcement Administration vanished as Tricia reappeared.

"I called the dining hall and put in a request for grits and eggs."

Jeremy's smile was dazzling. "What about bacon or sausage?"

A flash of humor crossed her face. "You really must be feeling good because there's nothing wrong with your appetite."

"I'd have to be dead not to eat."

She went completely still, her gaze fusing with his. "Please, Jeremy. Don't talk about dying." She didn't think she would ever forget the image of the tiny white coffin with their child being lowered into a grave.

He sobered quickly. "I'm sorry." He didn't know why he'd mentioned the word. He reflected again on the three members of his team who would never see their loved ones again. The jungle had claimed all of them.

The telephone rang, interrupting both their gloomy musings. Tricia straightened. "I'll answer it." Turning, she went back into the house and picked up the receiver to the phone on a side table in the entryway.

"Hello."

"Good morning, Tricia."

She recognized the distinctive drawling voice. "Good morning, Sheldon."

"How's Jeremy today?"

"He's sitting on the porch. I'm waiting for breakfast to be delivered."

"Good. I'm glad he's out of bed. Let him know

that Ryan just called with the news that Kelly had a little girl. Mother and baby are doing well.''

She bit down on her lower lip, remembering her own joy the instant she saw her daughter for the first time. "Congratulations, Sheldon.''

"Thank you. Please let Jeremy know that Sean and I will be over later this morning.''

"Okay.'' She hung up the phone, waiting until she was in control of her emotions, then returned to the porch.

One of the young men who worked in the dining hall had arrived and emptied a large wicker basket filled with serving dishes, a carafe of coffee and a pitcher of chilled orange juice onto the cloth-covered table on the porch.

"Thank you, Bobby,'' Tricia said, her soft voice breaking the silence.

Robert Thomas smiled at Tricia, blushing to the roots of his flaming red hair. "You're welcome, Miss Tricia. I'll pick up the dishes when I come back with lunch.''

Jeremy noticed the direction of the adolescent's gaze. It was fixed on Tricia's neckline. He'd told her about that doggone dress. Every time she inhaled or bent over the sight of her breasts made the flesh between his legs stir.

"Are you finished, Bobby?'' His voice snapped like the crack of a whip.

His head swiveling like Linda Blair's in *The Exorcist,* Bobby stared at Jeremy. "Yes, sir.''

"If that's the case, then beat it!"

Tricia opened her mouth to censure Jeremy for his rudeness, but the retort died on her tongue as she reminded herself that Jeremy was an owner of Blackstone Farms and Bobby an employee. She did not want to undermine Jeremy's authority in front of his workers.

Bobby managed to look embarrassed. "Yes, sir, Mr. Blackstone." Picking up the wicker basket, he made his way off the porch and raced to the SUV he had parked in the driveway.

Pulling out a chair, Tricia sat across the table from Jeremy. She uncovered a serving dish with fluffy scrambled eggs, another with steaming creamy grits and a third with a rash of bacon, spicy beef sausage links and strips of baked ham. She reached for his plate, filled it with grits and eggs and placed it in front of him.

"I didn't know bullying was a requisite for becoming a special agent with the DEA."

Jeremy's grip on his fork tightened. "What are you talking about?"

A slight frown marred her smooth forehead. "You didn't have to talk to Bobby like that." Bobby had been a toddler when she left the farm to attend college.

"It was either send him on his way or have him salivating over your cleavage."

Tricia placed a hand over her chest. "Do you have a problem with my dress?"

"It's not the dress, but what's in your dress." He lifted his eyebrows. "Or should I say what is spilling out of your dress."

She lowered her hand, deciding to ignore his ribald comment and served herself. "That was your father on the phone," she said, smoothly changing the topic. "Kelly had a girl, and both mother and baby are doing well."

Jeremy clenched his right fist. "Boo-yaw!"

Tricia felt his enthusiasm. "Congratulations, Uncle Jeremy."

He stared at her, his eyes brimming with tenderness. "Thank you, Tricia."

Her lower lip trembled as her mind fluttered in anxiety. She dropped her gaze and concentrated on the food on her plate, hoping to bring her fragile emotions under control because she had involuntarily reacted to Jeremy's gentle look.

She had told herself it wasn't going to work, and now she was certain. All Jeremy had to do was look at her with a gentle yearning and she was lost—lost in her own yearning that pulled her in and refused to let her go.

There was a time when he had become her knight in shining armor, protecting her from the taunts of the other farm children. He had taught her how to love herself and in turn she had fallen in love with him.

Tricia watched Jeremy as he attempted to feed himself. His right hand trembled noticeably and a muscle in his jaw twitched. She put down her fork. "Would you like something to take the edge off?"

Jeremy's head came up slowly. The blinding headache had returned. "I don't know."

"What don't you know?"

"I'm losing track of time. Whenever I wake up I don't know what day it is or whether it's day or night."

"Time should be the least of your concerns, Jeremy. You're not going anywhere for a while." She touched the corners of her mouth with a cloth napkin. "As soon as you're finished eating, I'll bring you your medication."

He nodded, then chided himself for the action. Each time he moved his head it felt as if it was going to explode.

Tricia aided Jeremy as he made his way over to a chintz-covered chaise at the opposite end of the porch. He lay motionless as she raised his injured foot to a pillow. She took his vitals and gave him the pill. Sitting on a matching rocker, she waited until his lids closed and his chest rose and fell in an even rhythm, indicating he had fallen asleep.

She sat, studying his face in repose, noting the lean jaw, aquiline nose and firm chin—features their daughter had inherited. Juliet had been a feminine version of her father with the exception of her mouth. Her mouth had been Tricia's.

She pushed off the rocker and began clearing the table. She washed the dishes, then carefully washed the china and silver and put them away. She returned to the porch, book in hand and sat down on the rocker.

The sound of an approaching vehicle shattered the stillness of the morning. Glancing up, she saw Sheldon's pickup truck maneuvering into the driveway. Tricia was on her feet, watching as Sheldon helped his grandson out of the truck. Sean Blackstone raced up the steps of the porch, his dark-gray eyes sparkling with excitement.

"I have a sister, Miss Tricia!" His high-pitched voice startled several birds perched on the branches of a nearby oak tree. They fluttered and chattered noisily before settling back under the cool canopy of leaves.

She stared down at the young boy, smiling. There was no doubt that he was Ryan's son. Tricia ruffled his black curly hair. "Congratulations on becoming a big brother."

"Daddy said I can't see my baby sister until she comes home with Mommy." Sean's gaze shifted, resting on his uncle on the chaise. "What happened to Uncle Jeremy, Miss Tricia? Why is his leg wrapped up like that?"

Tricia stared at Sheldon who now stood on the porch. It was obvious Sean hadn't been told about his uncle's injuries.

Resting a large hand on his grandson's shoulder, Sheldon let out his breath in an audible sigh. "Your uncle Jeremy had an accident. He fell and hurt his leg.''

Sean's head came up and he stared at Sheldon. ''Like a horse?''

Sheldon nodded. ''Yes, like a horse.''

''Grandpa, did he hurt his face when he fell down?''

''Yes, Sean. He also hurt his face when he fell,'' Sheldon said in a quiet voice. ''Why don't you go for a walk with Miss Tricia while I sit with Uncle Jeremy?''

Tricia reached for Sean's hand. ''Come with me. I'm going to see my grandfather.'' She knew Sheldon wanted to be alone with Jeremy, even though he was sedated.

''Take my truck, Tricia,'' Sheldon called out as he sat on the rocker she had just vacated. Everyone who lived or worked at the horse farm always left the keys in the ignition of their vehicles.

Tricia helped Sean into the pickup and belted him in before she sat behind the wheel and started the engine. It had been a while since she had driven a standard vehicle. She, like most of the children living at Blackstone Farms, had learned to drive a tractor as soon as their legs were long enough to reach the pedals.

She arrived at Gus's house and found his pickup missing. Turning to Sean, she smiled at him. ''How would you like to help me cut some flowers to make a bouquet for your mother and little sister to welcome them home?"

Sean flashed a wide grin. "Yes, Miss Tricia."

Fifty minutes later Tricia drove back to Jeremy's house with a basket filled with pink and white roses, a vase and spools of pink ribbon in varying shades. Her grandmother had taught her the intricacies of floral arranging. Tricia had also changed out of her dress and into a pair of black capris and a white camp shirt.

She stared at Jeremy. He was still asleep. "How was he?" she asked Sheldon in a quiet voice.

Sheldon cupped her elbow arm and led her away from where Sean sat next to his uncle. "He was talking in his sleep, Tricia."

Her heart stopped, then started up again. "What did he say?"

A knowing gaze pinned her to the spot. "He kept mumbling, 'I'm sorry, Tricia.'" A frown creased Sheldon's forehead. "What happened between you and my son?"

"I don't know what you're talking about."

Sheldon decided to be candid. "Were you the reason he joined the Marines instead of coming home?"

She met his accusing gaze without flinching. "I don't know why Jeremy joined the Marines. But, if you want answers as to what went on between me and Jeremy, then you're going to have to ask him."

Sheldon released Tricia's arm. He had many unanswered questions about Jeremy and Tricia's past relationship and he was determined to get some answers. He'd lost his son once, but he had no intention of losing him again.

He inclined his head. ''Thank you again for taking care of Jeremy. We'll talk about you and Jeremy later.''

She nodded, and, turning on his heel, Sheldon went to Sean and took his hand. Together they walked back to the truck.

Tricia stood watching uneasily until the departing vehicle disappeared from view.

Four

Tricia moved closer to Jeremy and held his uninjured hand as he sat on an examining table, while the nurse cut through the plaster cast on his ankle. The whirring sound of the drill set her teeth on edge. The plaster cast would be replaced with one made of fiberglass, but only after the removal of the surgical staples and an X-ray.

She noted the tense set of his jaw. "Are you all right?" she whispered close to his ear.

He turned his head, met her gaze and nodded. Their mouths were mere inches apart. His breath swept over her cheek. "Thank you for being here." Leaning forward, he brushed his mouth over hers with the softness of a breeze. There was no intimacy in the kiss, but that did not stop Tricia from reacting to the slight pressure. Unable to move, she felt her pulse race uncontrollably.

She wanted to tell Jeremy that she did not want to be here—with him—because with each sunrise it was becoming increasingly more difficult to sleep under his roof, to wake up and see him and not be affected by the sensual memories of what had been between them.

Jeremy stared at the rapidly beating pulse in Tricia's throat. He had only touched his lips to hers, when he'd wanted to do so much more. He wanted to ravish her mouth. He felt like a starving man craving food or a man dying of thirst needing water. He wanted to kiss her so badly.

He and Tricia could not go backward, yet despite her duplicity and infidelity he still wanted her. It no longer mattered that she had married or slept with other men. In spite of the anguish tormenting him for fourteen years he still wanted her in his bed.

He drew in a sharp breath with the removal of the first staple. A second one followed, then a third. He lost count of the biting sensation after fifteen. Closing his eyes, he rested his head against her shoulder. When the last staple was removed, he was helped into a wheelchair and pushed into another room where a technician X-rayed his hand and foot.

Tricia opened the passenger-side door, holding Jeremy's crutches. Moving slowly, he swung his legs around until his feet touched the macadam. She handed him the crutches and he pulled himself into a standing position.

It took him five minutes to make his way from the car to his bed, every step torture. He sat down heavily on the side of the bed and fell back on the mattress.

Tricia stood over him, hands on her hips. "I'm going to give you a pill."

Jeremy rested an arm over his forehead. "No, Tricia. I don't want it."

Reaching out, she placed her hand alongside his cheek. "Yes, Jeremy."

He caught her hand and kissed the palm. "Just let me rest for a little while."

"Are you sure?"

He smiled, the expression resembling a grimace. "Yes."

She eased her hand from his loose grip, removed his running shoe and the shapeless boot with Velcro fasteners from his injured foot, then raised his legs to the bed.

"I'll be nearby if you need me."

"Thank you, Tricia." He gave her a wry smile. "I seem to be thanking you a lot lately."

Tricia resisted the urge to kiss him, because at that moment he appeared boyish and carefree. The way she had remembered him. "Hush, now, and try to get some sleep."

Grinning, he saluted her. "Aye, aye, ma'am."

She sat on the club chair, slipped out of her sandals,

rested her bare feet on the ottoman and closed her eyes. She was exhausted. Jeremy rarely slept throughout the night and whenever he moaned or cried out in his sleep she left her bed to check on him. She always held him until he settled back to sleep, listening in shock as he mumbled about the horrors he had experienced during his ill-fated mission. These were the times when she felt like a voyeur. Willing her mind blank, she felt her chest rise and fall in an even rhythm, and she fell asleep.

Noise startled her, and she was jolted awake. Tricia sat up and stared at Jeremy. He was talking in his sleep again. She pushed up off the chair and sat on the side of the mattress.

"It's all right, Jeremy," she crooned softly.

"Forgive me, Tricia."

She leaned over him. "It's all right, darling. I forgive you."

"I…I did not want to…to leave…you," he mumbled, still not opening his eyes.

Getting into the bed with him, Tricia rested an arm over his chest, blinking back tears. "I love you," she whispered in his ear. Rising on an elbow, she kissed him.

Without warning Jeremy's eyes opened and he stared at her as if he had never seen her before. Tricia's heart beat a double-time rhythm. Had he heard her?

She met his questioning gaze. "You were talking in your sleep again."

"What did I say?"

She decided to tell him the truth. "You asked me to forgive you."

He closed his eyes, long black lashes resting on his high cheekbones. "For what?"

She hesitated and he opened his eyes. "For leaving me."

Jeremy's gaze fused with her dark-brown eyes. "I should've never left you, Tricia, but I took the coward's way out and ran, after Russell told me about the two of you."

She gasped, her mind reeling in confusion. Was that why he'd asked her if she had slept with Russell? Her breath burned in her throat as she swallowed the hateful words poised to explode from her mouth. They had wasted too many years, and she had lost a child because she'd refused to come back to the farm because of a spiteful man's lies.

"I don't care what Russell told you, but I never slept with him."

Jeremy's raven eyebrows lifted as he pushed up on an elbow. "He lied?"

"Of course he lied," she spat out. "Why didn't you ask *me,* Jeremy?"

A muscle quivered at his jaw. If he ever ran into Russell again he would make him sorry he ever drew breath. The SOB had lied to him about sleeping with Tricia.

"Why didn't you ask me?" she asked again.

Jeremy shook his head. He did not have an answer.

"I don't know. And don't think I haven't asked myself the same question over and over every time I came back here."

A look of distress crossed her face. "What hurts most is that you did not trust me. How could you profess to love me when you didn't trust me to be faithful to you?"

He frowned. "Loving you had nothing to do with not trusting you."

Tricia sat up. "Love *is* trust. You cannot have one without the other."

There was a prolonged silence before Jeremy said, "Do you still love me, Tricia?"

She felt as if all of her emotions were under attack and wanted to lie. But only minutes before she had openly confessed to loving him.

He had been her first lover, the man who unknowingly had made her a mother. She shook her head. "No," she said softly, "not the way I used to love you."

"Do you hate me?"

Smiling, Tricia shook her head again. "No, Jeremy, I don't hate you."

Sitting up, Jeremy shifted to his right side and kissed her. He inhaled the very essence of Tricia: her smell, the velvet softness of her mouth, the press of her breasts against his arm. He took his time kissing her mouth, eyes and face. She trembled when his lips brushed the curve of her eyebrows.

Tricia opened her mouth to his probing tongue,

swallowing his breath. What had begun as a soft, tender joining flowed into a dreamy intimacy she had forgotten existed.

Jeremy eased back, staring at her. "Do you know how long I've waited to kiss your mouth, eyes?"

Her gaze widened. "No." The single word was whispered.

"Forever," he whispered back, then took possession of her mouth again.

She emitted a soft moan. "We shouldn't be doing this."

"Why not?"

"Because I'm your nurse."

"That excuse is starting to sound lame," he crooned, gently biting her earlobe.

Tricia fortified herself against his sensual assault and placed a hand in the middle of his chest. "We can't go back to who we were. Too much time has passed and we're not the same people. I've changed and you've changed."

Reaching out, he pulled her effortlessly to sit on his lap, her back pressed to his chest. Her legs were cradled between his outstretched ones. "I don't want to go back, Tricia," he whispered in her ear. "Why can't we move forward?" He tightened his hold under her breasts.

A wave of desire flooded Tricia's body and she melted against the hardness of his chest. "That's not possible."

"Why not?"

"We don't have the time. I'm only going to be here for another three weeks."

Jeremy stared at the back of her head. He kissed her nape. "Three weeks is more than enough time." What he did not tell Tricia was that each hour, minute and second was precious, because he remembered counting down the seconds, minutes and hours while he and the others on his team lay waiting for death.

He wanted Tricia without a commitment or declaration of love. He wasn't ready to risk losing his heart to her again. "I've never asked anything from you, sweetheart," he continued, unaware that the endearment had slipped out, "not your love or your body. Those you gave willingly. What I am asking for is the next three weeks of your life."

Tricia was certain Jeremy could feel the flutters in her chest. "What happens after that?"

"Whatever it is you want to happen."

Shifting on his thighs, she turned in his loose embrace. His gaze was steady. "I'm leaving as planned on August fifteenth, so whatever we will share up to that time will become a part of our past."

Jeremy lifted his eyebrows. "Okay," he agreed. "When it comes time for you to leave I promise not to put any pressure on you to force you to stay."

Lowering her gaze, she smiled. "Thank you."

He angled his head and kissed her again. "Will you go out with me tonight?"

She gave him a sassy smile. "Are you asking me on a date?"

Pressing his forehead to hers, Jeremy flashed his brilliant white-toothed smile. "As a matter of fact, I am."

"Where do you want to go?"

"Out to dinner, then we'll take in a movie."

Tricia chuckled. "I believe we should begin with dinner. Sitting in a movie theater with your leg in a cast is a stretch."

Jeremy kissed the end of her nose. "I wasn't talking about a movie theater. We can eat out, then come back here and watch a movie."

He had used the home theater in the family room exactly twice since he'd purchased it two years before. A collection of DVDs stacked on several shelves were still in their original cellophane packaging. Whenever he came home on leave, he stayed in his house because he had come to value his privacy. But it had never felt like home...until now.

Curving her arms around his neck, Tricia rested her head on his shoulder. "You've got yourself a date. I'll call the dining hall and cancel dinner," she said, and rose to leave.

"And where do you think you're going?" he asked.

"I'm going over to my grandfather's to find something to wear."

Jeremy chuckled, the sound coming from deep within his chest. "I hope you're not going to wear that yellow dress."

Tricia gave him a long, penetrating stare. "What's with you and that dress?"

A sensual flame fired his eyes like flints of steel. "Nothing."

"If that's the case, then I'll wear it tonight."

His expression changed, becoming tight, strained. "Please don't, Tricia." He held up his left hand. "I still can't quite make a fist, so I won't be able to punch out some guy for leering at your breasts."

She sucked her teeth. "I thought you gave up brawling a long time ago."

"I did. Remember, the only times I got into fights were because of you."

Tricia ran a finger down the length of his nose seconds before she pressed her mouth to his. "I never wanted you to fight for me."

"Someone had to protect you."

"And you did, Jeremy." She'd lost count of the number of black eyes and bloody noses he had inflicted on a few of the farm kids. "I wrote in my diary that you were my knight in shining armor. I used to refer to you as Sir Blackstone, the Black Knight."

He nuzzled her neck. "Do you need my protection now?"

"No," she said in a quiet voice. "I've learned to protect myself." She slipped off the bed and put on her shoes. "Please stay in bed until I get back."

Jeremy's expression was one of faint amusement. He wanted to tell Tricia that he was quite capable of getting in and out of bed without her assistance as long as the crutches were within reach. Already he could groom and dress himself, navigate the stairs and feed himself. He still couldn't drive or walk distances, but, that would come in time.

He winked at her, then rested his head on the pillows and waited for her return.

When Tricia arrived at her grandfather's house, his truck wasn't in its usual parking space, which meant he was probably having dinner in the dining hall. The temporary solitude gave Tricia a chance to think about her relationship with her grandfather.

She usually visited with him every morning after Sheldon came to see Jeremy. She'd sit with Gus on the porch in easy silence. In the past, their relationship had been anything but easy. In fact, Gus still did not approve of her involvement with the owner's son. She wanted to tell Gus there was no need to torment himself about her and Jeremy because in three weeks she would leave Blackstone Farms, her ex-lover and return to her orderly life in Baltimore. However, this time when she left Virginia it would be without the tortured questions and memories.

She went into her bedroom and selected a black linen dress. Black lacy underwear and strappy black sling-back sandals completed her outfit. She showered, dressed, applied a light coat of makeup and set out for Jeremy's house. He was sitting on the porch waiting for her.

Her gaze raced over his off-white linen suit, matching shirt and tie. He wore the shapeless boot with Velcro fasteners and a black loafer. Walking slowly up the porch stairs, her gaze widened in appreciation. The light color of the suit was the perfect foil for his deeply tanned olive coloring.

Reaching for the crutches, Jeremy pulled himself up. "I thought I'd save some time and change before you got back."

She stared at his clean-shaven jaw. "I told you to wait for me."

Jeremy rested the crutches under his armpits. "I wasn't alone. Ryan came over with the baby. He left just before you drove up." A wide grin crinkled the skin around his luminous eyes. "Even though Vivienne is only a few days old, she's a beauty. She looks just like Kelly. To say that Ryan is a proud papa is putting it mildly," he said. "I don't remember Ryan being this excited when Sean was born."

Tricia returned his smile. "That's because this time he can really appreciate what it means to be a father."

"I guess you're right." He angled his head and looked her up and down, his gaze lingering on her long legs in the three-inch heels. "By the way, you look stunning."

She could not stop the heat from stealing into her cheeks. "Thank you."

Jeremy took a step. "Are you ready?"

Tricia nodded. "Yes."

She was ready, ready for Jeremy and the next three weeks.

Five

Tricia turned the key in the ignition, adjusted the air-conditioning, backed out of the driveway and drove along the main road that led away from Blackstone Farms.

She gave Jeremy a sidelong glance. ''Where are we going?''

''Take 64 to 81, then I'll tell you where to turn off.''

''How far is it from here?''

''About thirty clicks.''

She smiled. How could she have forgotten that Jeremy had been a Marine and was now a special agent with the DEA? The military jargon had just slipped out.

Nodding, she concentrated on driving instead of on the man sitting next to her. She had agreed to become involved with him again, but refused to think of the depth of their involvement. She doubted whether they would make love, because of his injury, but having an emotional relationship rather than a physical one was not an option either. If they became emotionally involved it would make their eventual separation that much harder…at least for her. Besides, it had been more than ten years since she had slept with a man.

Tricia increased her speed, passing the Blackstone property marker and headed for the interstate. Security devices and closed-circuit cameras mounted on poles and fences surrounding the horse farm monitored everyone entering or leaving the ten-thousand-acre compound.

Her narrowed gaze lingered on the dark clouds in the distance. "It looks like rain."

Jeremy studied the gunmetal-gray sky. A heat wave had held the Shenandoah Valley and the surrounding environs in a brutal grip for a month. Sheldon had ordered the trainers to limit most outdoor activities for the horses until the ninety-plus degrees and oppressive humidity eased, while in-ground sprinklers worked around the clock to keep the grazing pastures verdant.

"We need more than a passing thunderstorm," he stated matter-of-factly. As soon as the words were out of his mouth a roll of thunder shook the earth, followed by a flash of lightning that came dangerously close to the ground.

Tricia's jaw tightened as she stared straight ahead. The daytime running lights on her car shimmered eerily in the encroaching darkness. It was only minutes after seven.

"Pull off at the next exit," Jeremy ordered in a strained voice.

"Why?"

"Because I don't want you to drive."

She frowned. "But, you can't drive."

"I know I can't drive," he snapped angrily. "I'm not going to let you drive along a mountain road during a thunderstorm." Having grown up in the western part of the state, both Tricia and Jeremy knew of the number of accidents and fatalities that resulted from landslides and falling rocks during violent storms each year.

"Where do you want me to go?"

"I don't know. There's bound to be a motel close by."

Tricia left the interstate and drove along a county road. There came another roll of thunder, followed by lightning, then rain. Fat drops spattered the windshield.

Jeremy was hard-pressed not to tell Tricia to pull over on the shoulder and switch seats with him. Her car was an automatic and he didn't need his left foot to drive.

"Over there," he said, pointing to his right. A sign

advertising a bed-and-breakfast appeared out of no-where. The outline of a large white Victorian structure came into the sweep of the headlights.

Decelerating, Tricia maneuvered along a path leading to the Lind Rose bed-and-breakfast, parking under a porte cochere behind several SUVs. She cut off the engine, stepped out into the oppressive humidity and came around to assist Jeremy.

A side door to the three-story house opened and a tiny woman with short snow-white hair emerged. "Oh, you poor dears. Please come in out of the rain." The shadowy figure of a tall man joined her.

Tricia lagged behind Jeremy as he made his way toward the couple. He had left his jacket in the car, and despite the air-conditioning his shirt was pasted to his back. She felt her mouth go dry as she studied his broad shoulders under the finely woven shirt, the slimness of his waist and hips and long legs. His beautifully proportioned body equaled his classically handsome features.

"Welcome to the Lind Rose," a deep voice rumbled in the darkness. "I'm Lindbergh and this is my wife, Rose. We just heard on the scanner that the storm is a bad one. Hear tell a bridge near Craigsville was washed out, and the state police just shut down a portion of the interstate outside of Staunton."

Jeremy smiled at the tall gaunt man with a head of shocking white hair as he neared him. "I'm glad we stopped because we were planning to go through Craigsville."

"You're in luck tonight," Rose said, gesturing toward Jeremy's leg with the unattractive boot. "We happen to have a room on the first floor. Most folks who come here want to stay on the second or third floor because they want to sit out on the veranda and look at the mountains."

Jeremy nodded. "My wife and I need a room, and if it's not too late we'd also like to have dinner." The request had come out as if Jeremy had said it many times before.

Tricia stared at the smooth, taut, olive skin over the elegant ridge of his high cheekbones, her breath catching in her chest. He had referred to her as his wife.

Rose smiled. "Would you like to eat in the dining room or in your room?"

"The dining room."

"In our room." Tricia and Jeremy had spoken in unison as the older couple exchanged a knowing glance.

"Sweetheart, if it's all right with you I'd like to get off my feet," Jeremy said in a quiet tone.

Tricia wanted to glare and bare her teeth at him, but smiled sweetly instead. "Of course, *darling*. We'll dine in the room."

Reaching into his pocket, Jeremy withdrew a small leather case and extended it to Tricia. "Please take one of the cards." She reached for an American Express card and handed it to Rose. "We're also going to need some toiletries."

Rose gave the credit card to her husband. "All of the rooms come with baskets of complimentary grooming samples. You'll also find bathrobes and slippers. We ask that you leave them, but if you want them as souvenirs just let us know and we'll add the cost to your bill. Come with me and I'll show you your room."

Lindbergh stared at the name on the credit card before peering closely at Jeremy. "Are you one of those Blackstones from the horse farm?"

Jeremy's expression was impassive. "Yes."

Lindbergh reached for Jeremy's right hand and pumped it. "My pleasure, Mr. Blackstone." He nodded at Tricia. "Mrs. Blackstone."

"Let go of the man's hand, Lind," Rose admonished softly. "Don't you see he's hurting?"

Tricia moved closer to Jeremy and studied his face. Moisture dotted his forehead and his mouth was drawn into a tight line. There was no doubt he was uncomfortable.

He was in pain and his medication was back at the farm. She touched his shoulder. "Let's go to the room," she said softly.

Tricia and Jeremy followed Rose down a carpeted hallway to a room at the opposite end of the hall. Rose opened the door and flipped a wall switch. Table lamps filled the space with a warm, soft golden glow, highlighting an exquisite queen-size sleigh bed with a lace and organza coverlet and pillows. A table, doubling as a desk, held a vase of fresh white roses and a supply of candles next to a quartet of hurricane lanterns. The room also had a sitting area with a round table and two chairs, and an adjoining bathroom. Bundles of dried herbs lay on the grate in a stone fireplace instead of the usual logs.

Tricia smiled. "It's beautiful."

Rose beamed. "I'm glad you like it." She walked over to the table in the sitting area, picked up a small leather-bound binder and handed it to Tricia. "I'm certain we'll have most of what you'll need to make your stay comfortable. We also offer laundry service. If you want something washed, just put them in the bags you'll find on a shelf in the closet and hang it outside your door tonight. You'll also find today's menu in the binder. If there's anything you need other than what is listed, please let me or Lind know."

Walking slowly over to an overstuffed armchair, Jeremy sat down heavily. His ankle was throbbing. The orthopedist had warned him that atmospheric changes would affect the metal in his foot. He closed his eyes, praying the pain would go away.

Tricia placed her purse on a table near the bed and opened the binder. The entrées included roast chicken, filet mignon and broiled trout. The bed-and-breakfast also offered a variety of dishes for vegetarians and those on restricted diets.

"What do you want to eat?" she asked Jeremy.

He waved a hand, not opening his eyes. "Please order for me."

She spoke quietly with Rose, ordering the chicken

and fish entrées with steamed vegetables. Once Rose left to put in their order, she went over to Jeremy.

"Would you like to eat in bed?"

He opened his eyes and his head came up slowly. A slight smile played at the corners of his mouth. Had Tricia realized what she'd asked? Her naive question elicited erotic musings that made him temporarily forget about his pain. Yes, he wanted to eat in bed, taste every inch of her smooth fragrant skin from her face to her toes.

The notion of making love to her elicited a longing and a desire he had long thought dead. Whenever he made love to other women it was only for sexual release. But it had never been that way with Tricia. He hadn't consciously planned to seduce her, to get her into his bed, but the fact that they would share the same bed was now beyond her control, their control.

"Yes." The single word came out like a silken growl. His steady gaze met and fused with hers.

A minute passed before Tricia dropped her gaze. Turning on her heel, she went over to the bed, shifted the pillows and shams and turned back the coverlet. She went completely still when she registered the heat from Jeremy's body seeping into hers as he closed the distance between them. She shivered as his moist breath swept over the nape of her neck. She hadn't heard him get up.

"Help me into bed, sweetheart."

She took his crutches, propping them in a corner

as he sat down heavily on the mattress. Bending over, she removed his shoe. Her motions were measured, precise as she placed an arm under the back of his knees and lifted his legs onto the bed.

"Are you in pain?" she asked after he'd slumped back to the pillows.

"It's bearable."

"That's not what I asked."

He glared at her. "I said it's bearable."

She did not believe him, but decided not to press the issue. Reaching for the telephone on the nightstand, she dialed the number for room service. She would order something that would not only dull his pain but also his senses temporarily.

"This is Mrs. Blackstone. I'd like to order a bottle of Chardonnay." She ignored Jeremy's questioning look. "Yes. Thank you."

"When did you start drinking?" he asked after she ended the call.

At fifteen they'd taken two bottles of wine from the dining hall's wine cellar and finished one in less than an hour. Jeremy had been slightly tipsy while Tricia spent half the night in the bathroom, retching violently. Once she recovered she swore she would never drink again.

"I sometimes have a glass or two for special occasions."

He lifted an eyebrow. "Is this a special occasion?"

A smile softened her mouth. "I'd say it is."

His smile matched hers. "What are we celebrating?"

"A truce, Jeremy."

His smile faded. "I'd like to think of it as a reconciliation, *Mrs. Blackstone.*"

"Don't get carried away with yourself. I couldn't tell them I'm Miss Parker after you introduced me as your wife."

A muscle quivered at his jaw. "But you *could've* been Mrs. Blackstone."

She stared back at him for a long moment. "I could have been, but you chose to believe a lie."

Jeremy's eyes darkened with pain. Tricia did not know how many times he had punished himself for his cowardly actions. He'd run instead of staying to confront her. Even if she had lied about sleeping with Russell Smith, it still would have been better than not knowing.

"How long will I have to pay penance for deserting you, Tricia?"

"Fourteen years, Jeremy," she spat out angrily. "I loved you even when I became another man's wife. Every time he touched me I cursed you, because it was you I wanted to make love to, not Dwight. There were nights when I feigned sleep so I wouldn't have to make love with him. I punished Dwight when he didn't deserve to be punished." Her eyes glistened with unshed tears. "He was kind, patient but after a while even he couldn't put up with a cold and unresponsive wife."

Jeremy felt Tricia's pain as surely as if it was his own. He had hurt her—deeply. "I'm sorry. I know it sounds trite, but there's nothing else I can say. I'm sorry and I don't want you to leave the farm."

Straightening her spine, she stared down her nose at him. "What I promised to give you is three weeks. Please don't ask for more."

A sixth sense told him that something traumatic had happened to her during their separation. Something he knew he had to uncover before she left Blackstone Farms again.

He waited until Tricia walked into the bathroom, closing the door behind her, and leaned over to pick up the telephone receiver. He punched in several numbers. His call was answered after the third ring.

"Hey, Pop."

"Where the hell are you and Tricia?"

Jeremy ignored his father's sharp tone. "We're holed up at a bed-and-breakfast outside of Craigsville."

A heavy sigh came through the wire. "Dammit, Jeremy, you're going to put me in an early grave. Have you forgotten that everyone checks in during bad weather?"

Jeremy was aware of the mandated farm telephone chain that every resident check in with one another during violent weather.

"Half the county is blacked out because of downed power lines," Sheldon continued. "Poor Gus nearly passed out when I told him that I hadn't heard from you or Tricia.''

"Tell Gus Tricia is safe. We plan to spend the night here.''

There was a noticeable pause before Sheldon asked, "Is there something going on between you and Gus's granddaughter?''

Jeremy hesitated, then said, "Yes, Pop. There's something going on between Tricia and me, but it's something we have to work out by ourselves.''

"I asked Tricia if she was the reason you joined the Marine Corps instead of coming back to the farm and she said I had to ask you.''

"Since you've asked, I'll give you an answer. I ran away instead of confronting her about something someone told me.''

"Are you still running, son?''

Jeremy smiled. "No, Pop.''

"Does this mean I can retire?''

"No. You're too young to retire.''

"I'm tired, Jeremy. Thirty years in this business is enough. Now all I want to do is fish and spoil my grandchildren.''

Jeremy closed his eyes and took a deep breath. "Can we talk about this another time?''

There was silence before Sheldon said, "Sure.''

"Good night, Pop.'' He hung up the phone at the same time Tricia walked out of the bathroom.

"Who were you talking to?''

"My father. I called to let him know we're safe. He'll let your grandfather know that we're together."

Tricia nodded. It was one thing to sleep under Jeremy's roof and another to sleep with him—in the same bed—at a bed-and-breakfast. She did not have to be a clairvoyant to know Gus Parker's thoughts once Sheldon told him she and Jeremy were spending the night together away from the farm. Her grandfather had warned her repeatedly not to become involved with Jeremy…and she knew instinctively his warning had something to do with her mother.

Every time she'd asked her grandparents about her father they went mute. Had Patricia Parker become involved with someone who had been a boss's son?

Reuniting with Jeremy had changed her because she now had answers to her past—all but the identity of her father. As soon as she returned to Blackstone Farms she intended to confront her grandfather about her mother *and* her father.

Tricia sat down on a chair beside the bed and stared at Jeremy. He lay, his head and shoulders cradled on a mound of pillows, staring up at the ceiling. A comfortable silence filled the space as the sound of rain lashed at the windows. She moved off the chair when a knock on the door signaled the arrival of their dinner.

Six

Tricia turned off the lamp and slipped under the cool crisp sheet. The heat from Jeremy's nude body was overwhelming as he shifted on his side and rested an arm over her bare hip.

He nuzzled her ear. "How are you feeling?"

She smiled in the darkness. She could not remember the last time she'd felt so relaxed. "Wonderful. Why?"

Jeremy chuckled. "I don't want to take advantage of you if you're under the influence." He had drunk three glasses of wine to her two.

Turning to face him, Tricia looped an arm over his shoulder. "You're in no condition to talk trash, hotshot. Especially not with a busted ankle."

"My busted ankle has nothing to do with my ability to make love to you," he countered softly.

She snuggled against his chest. "Go to sleep, Jeremy."

"I don't think so."

Tricia went completely still. "You're kidding, aren't you?"

"No," he whispered against her moist parted lips. "I want you."

Pulling out of his embrace, she sat up and turned on the lamp on her side of the bed. Her heart fluttered wildly in her chest when she saw the direction of Jeremy's gaze. He was staring at her breasts, and she resisted the urge to pull the sheet up to her neck.

"I'm not going to lie and say I don't want you," she whispered. "But…" Her words trailed off.

He pushed up on an elbow. "But what, Tricia?"

She bit her lower lip. "Making love will complicate things."

"What things?"

"My having to leave you."

Jeremy held her gaze. "Didn't I tell you that I wouldn't try to pressure you to stay?"

When it comes time for you to leave I will not put any pressure on you to force you to stay. His declaration had stayed with Tricia, she wanted to believe him.

"You promise?" Her voice was soft, childlike.

"Have I ever lied to you, Tricia?"

A smile trembled over her lips. "No, Jeremy. You've

never lied to me." Leaning forward, she kissed him, her lips caressing his. "No," she whispered over and over as she kissed his chin, jaw and forehead. Moving over him, she lay between his legs and kissed every inch of his face before her tongue mapped a path down his chest to his flat belly.

Jeremy felt a swath of heat race down his body. It settled in his groin, and his sex hardened quickly. He had waited years, more than a decade to experience the unrestrained, uncontrollable desire Tricia wrung from him. While he lay hidden in a swamp in a South American jungle he'd thought of her and the times they'd made love. He had forced himself to remember all of the good times in his life while he awaited death either from venomous insects, reptiles or the men searching for the team of DEA agents who'd inadvertently stumbled upon their cocaine factory.

He closed his eyes, curled his fingers into a fist and reveled in the sensual waves rippling up and down his body, letting his senses take over. He heard the rain slashing at the windows, felt the sweep of Tricia's breasts as she slid down his body and inhaled the fragrance of her perfume mingling with the rising scent of her desire. He did not know how, but he'd always been able to detect desire rising from the pores of her velvety skin.

Tricia had confessed to wanting him, even though she'd married another man, and it had been the same for him. Every woman he'd ever known had become Tricia Parker.

Unclenching his hands, he reached down and pulled her up before he climaxed. What he wanted—more than anything—was to explode inside her hot fragrant body.

Tricia tried freeing herself from Jeremy's grip, but she was no match for his superior strength as she lay over his chest. The soft light from the lamp spilled over his features. His eyes were dark and unfathomable.

"Sit on me," he ordered quietly.

She shook her head. "No, Jeremy. I don't want to hurt you."

He covered a breast with his hand, measuring the shape and weight of the full, ripe globe. His thumb made sweeping motions over the nipple. It hardened quickly.

"Another part of my body is hurting right now, and it's definitely not my foot."

Tricia knew if she permitted Jeremy to penetrate her without using protection, then there was the possibility of her becoming pregnant. She could not forget how easily she had conceived a child with him fourteen years before.

She shook her head again. "Not without protection, Jeremy."

His mouth twitched in amusement. "There are condoms in the bathroom."

Her jaw dropped. "You brought condoms with you?"

Jeremy was amused by her reaction. "No. There

are a few in my grooming basket. Either you get them or hand me the crutches and I'll get them.''

Tricia leaned closer and pressed her breasts to his chest. The strong, steady pumping of his heart echoed hers. ''Let me make love to you without you penetrating me,'' she whispered close to his ear.

He smiled. ''The next time you can make love to me. Tonight we'll make love to each other. I want to be inside you.''

Tricia wanted Jeremy inside her, so deep he touched her womb, deep enough to make her sob in ecstasy as he'd done when she was a girl. She wanted him so deep inside her that they'd cease to exist as separate entities. But as much as she wanted Jeremy, Tricia feared becoming pregnant again.

''Please don't make me beg, sweetheart,'' Jeremy whispered.

He was asking what she'd wanted for years, what she wanted each time she'd permitted her ex-husband to make love to her. She'd spent years since she'd left the farm fantasizing about sleeping with Jeremy, and now that she was given a second chance she found herself balking.

She'd had and lost their baby. In that instant, Tricia vowed that if she were to become pregnant again, this time she would tell Jeremy. She kissed him deeply, her tongue meeting and curling around his in a sensual dance of desire.

''Don't go away. I'll be right back.''

Jeremy's gaze followed her as she slipped off the

Play the Lucky Hearts Game

and get...
2 FREE BOOKS
and a FREE MYSTERY GIFT...
YES! YOURS to KEEP!

I have scratched off the silver card. Please send me my *2 FREE BOOKS* and *FREE mystery GIFT*. I understand that I am under no obligation to purchase any books as explained on the back of this card.

Scratch Here!
then look below to see what your cards get you...
2 Free Books & a Free Mystery Gift!

326 SDL D34S

225 SDL D349

FIRST NAME   LAST NAME

ADDRESS

APT.#   CITY

STATE/PROV.   ZIP/POSTAL CODE   (S-D-10/04)

Twenty-one gets you
2 FREE BOOKS
and a *FREE MYSTERY GIFT!*

Twenty gets you
2 FREE BOOKS!

Nineteen gets you
1 FREE BOOK!

TRY AGAIN!

The Silhouette Reader Service™ — Here's how it works:

BUSINESS REPLY MAIL

FIRST-CLASS MAIL   PERMIT NO. 717-003   BUFFALO, NY

POSTAGE WILL BE PAID BY ADDRESSEE

SILHOUETTE READER SERVICE
3010 WALDEN AVE
PO BOX 1867
BUFFALO NY 14240-9952

NO POSTAGE
NECESSARY
IF MAILED
IN THE
UNITED STATES

If offer card is missing write to: The Silhouette Reader Service, 3010 Walden Ave., P.O. Box 1867, Buffalo, NY 14240-1867 bed and made her way to the bathroom. She had gained weight in all the right places. Her body was full and voluptuous. It reminded him of lush, sweet overripe fruit. Tricia's footfalls were silent as she returned to the bed. Extending her hand, she dropped a small square packet onto his chest.

Smiling, Jeremy picked it up and tore open the foil covering and took out the latex sheath. "Can you please put it on?" He held it up with his injured left hand.

Tricia rested her hands on her hips, her eyes narrowing. "You're really pushing it, aren't you?"

He lifted a raven eyebrow. "It's your call, Tricia. It wouldn't bother me if you rode bareback."

She shook her head. "No, Jeremy. I can't afford to get pregnant."

Jeremy sobered and pushed himself into a sitting position. "You know I always wanted you to be the mother of our children."

What Tricia wanted to tell him was that she'd had his child—a daughter who'd looked so much like him. Taking the condom, she slipped it on. She had barely completed the task when she found her face pressed to Jeremy's hard shoulder, his hand cupping the back of her head.

She felt like crying as she wound her arms around his neck. Easing back, she kissed him tentatively, inhaling his breath and masculine scent. He'd just echoed what lay in her heart.

"Don't talk, Jeremy. Just love me," she whispered,

repeating the entreaty she'd uttered the last time they'd made love.

Jeremy's hands moved up and down her back, his fingertips trailing over her skin until she shuddered and moaned softly. He loathed the temporary disability that would not let him move and become an active participant; he wanted to use every inch of the large bed, trail his tongue along the length of Tricia's spine and he wanted to bury his face between her scented thighs and sample her feminine nectar. But more than anything he wanted to sheath his flesh inside her, feel her moist heat, the orgasmic convulsions that never failed to bring him to a free fall that would make him forget everything except Tricia.

Tricia took her time reacquainting herself with her ex-lover's body. She kissed his ear before tracing its shape with her tongue. She placed light kisses over the curve of his arching eyebrows, pressed her lips to the pulse in his throat, ran the tip of her tongue around the circle of his nipples until he moaned deep in his chest.

What had begun as slow, seductive foreplay turned into a sensual dance of desire. She lost track of time and place as her blood raced through her veins. As Jeremy became more aroused she felt herself losing control. Shifting, she fitted her hips over his.

A slight gasp escaped Tricia as Jeremy raised his hips off the mattress and he stared at the shocked expression on her face. She was as tight as she had been as a virgin, and he wondered how long had it been since she'd slept with a man.

He cradled her bottom. ''Do it slow. That's it,'' he urged as she lowered herself, inch by inch over his aroused flesh. It was his turn to gasp as her tight, hot walls closed around him. They moaned in unison once he was buried inside her.

Bracing her hands on his shoulders, Tricia stared at Jeremy staring up at her. She moved slowly at first, then quickened her motions when he cupped her breasts, squeezing them gently. There had been a time when Jeremy's hands could easily cover her breasts, but that time had passed. Pregnancy and breast-feeding had sensitized her nipples and increased her bust size from a 34B to a 38D.

Hypnotized by his touch, she trembled under his fingertips and closed her eyes as her body vibrated with a fire that threatened to ignite her into a million pieces where she would never be whole again.

Jeremy let go of Tricia's breasts and curved his arms around her waist until she lay flush on him. Her soft moans of pleasure against his ear became his undoing. He arched his hips, meeting her as she rose and fell over his rigid flesh, the flames of passion burning hot—hotter than it had ever been for them.

This truce, their reconciliation had become a raw act of possession as he sought to leave his brand not only on her body but also in her heart. Silently, wordlessly he implored her to stay.

He closed his eyes, gritting his teeth as Tricia's

flesh convulsed around him, she moaning softly as liquid heat flowed from her. Seconds later he abandoned himself to the rush of pleasure that left him weak and light-headed.

Jeremy emitted a low, guttural moan as Tricia's still-pulsing flesh milked the remnants of his release. He tightened the hold on her waist, not wanting to move or let her go.

He felt like a hypocrite. He'd sworn an oath to bring to justice those who sold drugs. Meanwhile, he had become addicted not to illegal substances but to a woman. Tricia had become his drug of choice.

"Jeremy?"

Her husky voice broke into his musing. "Yes, baby?"

"Did I hurt you?"

Turning his head, he dropped a kiss on her damp curly hair. "No, darling. Did I hurt you?"

"No." Tricia had told him no even though she knew she would probably experience some discomfort in a few hours. Muscles she hadn't used in years were certain to be tender.

He kissed her forehead. "How long has it been?"

She knew he wanted to know how long had it been since she'd shared her body with another man. She waited a full minute, then said, "Ten years."

Staring up at the ceiling, he cursed mutely, cursed the time they'd been apart and cursed his own pigheadedness.

* * *

The rain stopped an hour before dawn, and it was late morning when Tricia finally maneuvered into the driveway leading to Jeremy's house. The storm had downed tree limbs and scattered debris for miles. She came to a complete stop as a tall figure rose from a chair on the porch. Sheldon had been waiting for them.

She glanced at Jeremy's stoic expression. ''I'm going over to see my grandfather and get a change of clothes.'' Not waiting for a reply, she got out, retrieved the crutches resting behind the rear seats and handed them to Jeremy, who anchored them against his ribs.

Lowering his head, he brushed a kiss over her mouth. ''I'll see you later.'' He stood motionless, watching as she got back into the car and drove away, then turned and stared up at his father. Sheldon leaned against a porch column, arms crossed over his chest.

''What's up, Pop?''

Sheldon's expression was a mask of stone. ''Nothing.''

Jeremy slowly made his way up the porch steps and sat down on the chaise. ''I told you last night Tricia and I were okay.''

Pushing off the column, Sheldon pulled over a rocker to face his son. He sat down and clasped his large hands together. ''I wanted to see for myself that you were all right.''

''You used to say that when I was fifteen. Have you forgotten how old I am?''

Sheldon's expression was one of pained tolerance. "I know how old you are, Jeremy," he snapped.

"What's this all about, Pop?"

"It's about me being a father, Jeremy." He frowned, his steely eyes shooting off angry sparks. "It's about me worrying about my son, and if I live to be ninety and you're seventy I still have the right to worry. It comes with the territory. But that's something you wouldn't understand because of your selfishness. You left here at eighteen, and over the past fourteen years you've become a drifter. You're here for a day or two, then you're gone.

"Half the time I don't know where you are or whether you're dead or alive. Every night I say a prayer of thanksgiving because someone from the Justice Department did not show up with an announcement that my son died in the line of duty."

A shadow of annoyance tightened Jeremy's features. "If you're trying to make me feel guilty about my career choice, then forget it."

"It's not about guilt, Jeremy. It's about being responsible. I've worked my ass off for the past thirty years to make this horse farm a success, because I wanted to give you and Ryan things I didn't have. I'm retiring next year whether you stay on or not. And if Ryan isn't able to hold everything together, then I'm going to sell the farm."

Jeremy stared at Sheldon, complete surprise on his face. "You can't sell it."

Sheldon angled his head and lifted his eyebrows. "You think not?"

"But you promised my mother on her deathbed that you'd never sell the farm." It was with Julia's inheritance and her urging that prompted Sheldon to purchase his first Thoroughbred.

"Your mother's gone and I'm here," Sheldon countered as he rose to his feet.

Shock quickly turned to fury as Jeremy glared at his father's retreating back. He resented Sheldon's attempt to pressure him to give up his law enforcement career with the DEA.

He sat on the chaise recalling his passionate encounter with Tricia, temporarily forgetting Sheldon's threat to sell Blackstone Farms.

Three weeks.

The two words nagged at Jeremy because, after recapturing the passion that had eluded him for years, he had to ask himself if he was prepared to lose Tricia a second time.

Seven

Tricia walked into Gus's house with a determined stride. It had been years since she'd asked her grandfather about her parents, and his answer had always been "Let sleeping dogs lie."

Well, she was ready to wake up the dogs and didn't care whether they barked, snarled or bit. She was thirty-two years old—old enough to accept the truth no matter how shocking or painful.

"Grandpa," she called out as she walked through the living room. Bright sunlight coming through the windows revealed a light layer of dust on the coffee table. She made a mental note to come by later to dust and vacuum. It had been her grandmother who had kept the house immaculate.

Gus wasn't there even though his truck was parked in its usual spot. Shrugging a shoulder, Tricia showered and dressed. Jeremy was scheduled to see a psychiatrist later in the afternoon. She lingered long enough to tape a note on the refrigerator for Gus to call her at Jeremy's house. They had to arrange a time to sit down and *talk.*

Tricia sat in the doctor's waiting room, flipping through magazines as she waited for Jeremy. She glanced surreptitiously over the magazine at a woman who had tried unsuccessfully to calm her young son. He talked incessantly while fidgeting. The boy ignored his mother, sliding off his chair and onto the floor. His motions mimicked making a snow angel. There was no doubt the child was there to be evaluated for ADHD: attention deficit hyperactivity disorder. She smiled at the boy as he got up and approached her. His dark eyes gleamed and he returned Tricia's smile.

She was surprised when he sat down next to her, and she surmised he was either four or five. Reaching for one of the books stacked on a nearby table, he handed it to her.

"Read," he ordered in a manner that said he was used to being obeyed.

The book was Dr. Seuss's *Green Eggs and Ham.* She opened to the first page and began reading. The little boy sat quietly, listening to her soft voice as she read the entire book. She closed it, glanced up and saw Jeremy leaning on his crutches. He stared at her with a strange expression on his face.

Handing the book back to the child, she smiled. "I have to go now."

The boy pointed at Jeremy. "Is he your father?"

Tricia laughed. Jeremy certainly did not look old enough to be her father. "No, he isn't."

"What is he?"

She took a quick glance at Jeremy, who'd raised his eyebrows in a questioning gesture. "He's my—"

"I'm her boyfriend," Jeremy said. Taking in her annoyed expression, he smiled for the first time since he'd entered the medical building. Tricia seemed so at ease with the child. There was no doubt she was a wonderful pediatric nurse and probably would have been an excellent pediatrician.

His smile faded. His session with the psychiatrist had not gone well. The doctor had asked him questions he could not and did not want to answer. Jeremy was certain that a copy of the doctor's evaluation of his condition would be faxed to Special Operations in Washington, D.C., and placed in his personnel file.

Tricia stood up and walked over to him. "Are you ready?"

He did not move. "Am I, Tricia?" he asked softly.

"Are you what?"

"Your boyfriend?"

"Definitely not. You're my patient," she answered.

Jeremy stiffened as if Tricia had struck him, and a shadow of annoyance crossed his face seconds before he walked to the door. He paused as she held the door open for him, then he made his way down a ramp to where she had parked her car.

Waiting until she was seated behind the wheel, he turned and glared at her. "What am I to you, Tricia?"

Taken aback by the question, she stared at him with wide eyes. "Let it go, Jeremy."

"I don't want to let it go," he countered, his voice rising slightly.

"If you're looking to argue with me, then you're out of luck today."

Jeremy refused to relent. He had to know where he stood with her. "I don't intend to argue, Tricia. Just answer the question."

There was one thing she knew and remembered about Jeremy and that was his stubborn streak. Once he believed in something, no one could get him to change his mind. He'd believed Russell Smith's lie about them sleeping together and in the end it had cost them a future together.

"You're someone I grew up with and slept with, someone to whom I gave my heart and innocence, someone I fell in love with, someone who did not trust me enough to believe I'd be faithful. And I am someone who on August fifteenth will get into my car and drive back to Baltimore and the life I've made for myself." She took a deep breath. "Does that answer your question, Jeremy?"

A lethal calmness shimmered in the dark-gray eyes that held her gaze. "Yes, Tricia, it does."

* * *

The ride back to the farm was accomplished in complete silence. Tricia hadn't turned on the radio and with each passing mile the silence swelled until it was deafening.

She didn't know what Jeremy wanted from her. He'd asked her to forgive him, and she had. They'd reconciled, made love and chances were they would continue to sleep together up until the time her vacation ended. Jeremy said he wouldn't pressure her to stay, but he also hadn't offered her anything that would give her a reason to stay.

She drove through the electronic gate and maneuvered onto the road where several Thoroughbreds grazed behind a fence. Slowing, she came to a complete stop. Her gaze was glued to a small figure sitting astride a magnificent black horse racing around the winding, muddy track. Three men stood outside the fence screaming at the top of their lungs, while a fourth sat on the top rail, holding a stopwatch. Tricia's breath caught in her throat.

"Oh—" Jeremy swallowed an expletive as he watched jockey and horse become one as they appeared to fly over the track. His heart was pounding in his chest by the time horse and rider crossed the finish line. A loud roar rent the air. The jockey jumped off and pumped a gloved fist in the air.

Tricia stared numbly as the jockey took off his headgear and a tumble of dark hair floated around his shoulders. It wasn't until he turned that she realized he was a she.

She turned and stared at Jeremy, the pulse in her throat fluttering wildly. This is what she'd missed about Blackstone Farms: the excitement of prerace activity.

"Who is she?"

"Her name is Cheryl Carney, also known as Blackstone Farms' secret weapon. She's Kevin Manning's niece. Pop claims she's a horse whisperer and that she and Shah Jahan can communicate telepathically." Kevin Manning had taken over as head trainer after Russell Smith's father moved his family to the West Coast.

"Has Jahan raced competitively yet?" Tricia asked when she recalled the celebration following the ebony colt's birth.

"Not yet. Pop wants to wait until he's two. He's still too skittish to compete because whenever he's on the track with another horse he has to wear blinkers."

"There's no doubt he's destined for greatness."

Jeremy nodded. "Ryan predicts that if he stays healthy, then he'll become the farm's first potential Triple Crown winner."

Tricia raised her eyebrows. "He's that good?"

"With Cheryl riding him there's no doubt he'll become a winner." You and I were that good, he added silently.

Tricia shifted into gear and drove past the stables. She never realized how much she missed the horse farm until she returned. The smell of horseflesh, hay and fields of heather and lavender growing in the undeveloped north end of the property were like an aphrodisiac. She visited on average of twice a year: summer and winter. This was the first time she had decided to spend an entire month.

She drove past the schoolhouse made up of four connecting buildings. She thought about Jeremy's offer to become a school nurse and quickly dismissed it. It wasn't that being a school nurse would be unrewarding. It was just that she enjoyed working with the four pediatricians who had set up one of the largest practices in downtown Baltimore.

"Do you miss the farm, Tricia?"

Jeremy had read her mind. "Yes, I do," she answered truthfully.

"What do you miss most?"

She gave him a quick glance. "The people. They're like my extended family. I may have been an only child, but I fought and argued with the other kids as if we were brothers and sisters."

Jeremy nodded, smiling. He had become known as the Blackstone brawler. At that time it was not in his psychological makeup to walk away from a fight, and the number of encounters escalated after his mother's death. He'd been filled with rage because Julia had chosen to hide her illness from everyone until it was too late for her to seek medical treatment.

Resting his left arm over the back of Tricia's seat,

his fingers feathered through the soft curls on the nape of her neck.

"Could you please drop me off at Ryan's."

She made a right turn and less than a minute later she maneuvered into the driveway to Ryan and Kelly's home. Tricia parked, got out of the car and handed Jeremy his crutches.

"Aren't you coming in?" he asked as she turned to get back into the vehicle.

She shook her head. "No."

Jeremy studied her thoughtfully. "Don't you want to see the baby?"

Tricia forced a smile she did not feel. "I'll see her another time." Interacting with newborns was something she did often, but it would be different with Vivienne. She was a Blackstone, Sheldon's granddaughter, just like Juliet, and the image of Juliet's tiny lifeless body was still imprinted on her mind. Even after so many years, that image was still painful for Tricia to bear.

She wondered if she would be able to cradle Vivienne and successfully hold back tears and not relive the joy of becoming a mother and the pain of burying a part of herself. And she knew the answer before she had formed the question—no, not yet.

"I have to talk to my grandfather about something." Tricia glanced at her watch. "I'll come back at six to pick you up for dinner."

"Where would you like to eat tonight?"

"The dining hall," she said quickly.

Jeremy's dark eyebrows slanted in a frown. He did not want to eat at the farm. He wanted a repeat of what he and Tricia had had the night before.

"We can eat at the dining hall tomorrow night." There was a thread of hardness in his statement.

"You asked me where I wanted to eat and I said the dining hall," Tricia retorted.

He refused to relent. "Perhaps I should've said that we *are* eating out tonight."

Tricia reacted quickly to the challenge in his voice. "Perhaps not, Jeremy." She gave him a hostile glare. "Let me remind you that I don't work for *you*. Your father asked me to help you. He asked, not demanded, Jeremy. If you want me to do something, then I suggest you ask politely."

Not giving him the opportunity for a comeback, Tricia got into the car and drove away. She glanced into the rearview mirror and found him leaning on his crutches. His image stayed with her even after she'd walked into Gus's house and found him sitting in his favorite chair, dozing.

Why didn't I wait until he got into the house? What if he had fallen trying to make it up the porch steps?

Concern for Jeremy continued to haunt her until she shook Gus gently to wake him. Gus's eyes opened and he seemed surprised to see her.

"Grandpa, you shouldn't sleep sitting up. It's not good for your circulation."

Gus affected a slow smile. "Don't worry yourself

about me, baby girl. Since I stopped salting my food, my ankles don't swell up like they used to.''

Tricia held out a hand. ''Come sit with me on the love seat. I want to talk to you about something.''

''I saw your note.''

''Did you call me?''

Shaking his head slowly, Gus said, ''No, because I know what it is you want to talk about.''

''I need answers.''

''Let it go, Tricia.''

''I can't, Grandpa. I'm not a little girl. I'm a grown woman. I have a right to know something about my mother and my father.''

Gus closed his eyes. ''Let sleeping dogs lie, Tricia.''

''I can't and I won't!''

He opened his eyes and stared up at her, and it was then Tricia realized she had yelled at her grandfather. A strange expression crossed his face seconds before he placed a gnarled hand over his chest and slumped forward, his chin resting on his chest.

Tricia was galvanized into action. She caught Gus's wrist, measuring his pulse. It was slow, weak.

Somehow she managed to get him off the chair and onto the floor and began cardiopulmonary resuscitation. Each time she compressed his chest, she prayed, Please don't let him die.

Ryan opened the door for Jeremy. His expression registered shock seeing his brother standing on his porch—alone. ''How did you get here?''

"Tricia drove me."

Peering around Jeremy's shoulder, Ryan asked, "Where is she?"

"She went to see her grandfather. Are you going to let me in, or are you going to wait for me to fall?"

Ryan, deciding to ignore Jeremy's acerbic tone, took a step backward and opened the door wider. "Please enter, sir prince."

Jeremy rolled his eyes at his older brother and made his way slowly into the living room. He sat down on a deep club chair, placed his crutches on the floor and raised his left leg onto a footstool.

Ryan sat in a facing armchair and ran a hand over his close-cropped hair. "If you've come to see Kelly and the baby, you're out of luck because they're napping. However, if you've come to bitch and moan, then I'm all ears."

Jeremy frowned. "Who's bitching and moaning?"

"Pop."

"What's up with him?"

Ryan hesitated, then said, "You are."

Jeremy groaned softly. "What now?"

"He's going to sell the farm."

"Sell or he's threatening to sell?"

Ryan's expression was a mask of stone. "Sell, Jeremy!"

"Pop is being manipulative."

"Wrong. Pop is being Pop. I told you last year that he's tired."

Jeremy frowned in cold fury. "I know what

brought on his tirade.'' He revealed to Ryan what he and Sheldon had talked about after he and Tricia returned from spending the night at the bed-and-breakfast.''

A slow smile formed on Ryan's lips. ''You and Tricia Parker?''

Jeremy smiled in spite of himself and nodded. ''Yeah.''

''Damn, brother, you sure had me fooled. I thought you and Tricia were just good friends.''

''We started out as friends, but the year we turned eighteen something happened.''

''Was that little something called love?''

Before Jeremy could answer Ryan's query, the telephone rang. Reaching for the phone on a nearby table, Ryan spoke softly into the mouthpiece. His expression changed as he stood up. ''Stay with him, Tricia. I'll be right there as soon as I call the hospital. No, don't try to move him.'' He depressed a button, then two others. The speed dial connected him to the local hospital.

Jeremy reached down for his crutches and was on his feet the moment he heard his brother mention ''possible heart attack,'' and Augustus Parker's name.

''I'm coming with you,'' he said.

''Try to keep up,'' Ryan said over his shoulder as he raced out of the house.

Eight

"**S**top beating up on yourself," Jeremy whispered to Tricia for what seemed like the hundredth time since Gus Parker was wheeled into the emergency room.

She closed her eyes and rested her head on his shoulder. "I should never have argued with him."

Jeremy tightened his grip around her waist as they sat together on a love seat in a waiting area. "You snapped at me earlier about ordering you about, and now I'm going to do exactly that. I want you to stop blaming yourself for Gus's heart attack. If it hadn't happened now, there's nothing to say it wouldn't have happened after your return to Baltimore. Gus seeing your face once he comes out of surgery is certain to lift his spirits."

Tricia nodded. She opened her eyes to find Sheldon sitting several feet away staring at her and Jeremy. Ryan had driven Gus to the hospital and stayed to confer with the cardiologist who was scheduled to perform open-heart surgery. Ryan then called Sheldon and informed him of Gus's condition. Sheldon had driven from the farm to the hospital in record time.

Pushing off his chair, Sheldon stood up. "I'm going to get some coffee. Would either of you like some?"

Jeremy straightened and removed his arm from Tricia's waist. "How do you want yours?"

Tricia seldom drank coffee, but this was one time when she needed a jolt from the caffeine. "Black."

"Make that two blacks, Pop."

Waiting until Sheldon walked away, Jeremy leaned closer to Tricia, held her hand and pressed a kiss to her cheek. "He's going to be all right." Gus had been in surgery for more than two hours.

Turning her head, she smiled at him. "I want to thank you for being here for me."

"There's…"

The cardiologist walked into the waiting room preempting whatever it was Jeremy planned to say. Tricia stood up on trembling legs as Jeremy came to his feet.

She bit down on her lower lip, gathering courage. "How is my grandfather?"

He offered her a comforting smile. "He has been stabilized and is in the intensive care unit."

"When can I see him?"

"Not until tomorrow."

A flicker of apprehension coursed through Tricia. "What aren't you telling me, Dr. Lawrence?"

"It's apparent your grandfather suffered a mild heart attack in the past which weakened the heart wall. He's going to have to take it easy so the muscles can heal."

"My grandfather never had a heart attack," she argued softly.

"Perhaps he'd experienced chest pains in the past but ignored them. But I can assure you that there is evidence of some heart damage."

"How long will Mr. Parker have to remain in the hospital?" Jeremy asked as he moved closer to Tricia's side.

"At least a week," Dr. Lawrence replied, "followed by a minimum of six weeks of limited activity. After he's reevaluated, then he will have to undergo physical therapy that will help him regain some endurance." He stared at Tricia. "Is there someone at home who can take care of him?"

"I'll take care of him," she said, not hesitating. Her grandfather's heart attack meant she would not return to Baltimore as planned. "I'm going to need medical documentation to take Family Leave."

"You can pick up a form at the business office in the morning." The cardiologist patted her shoulder. "Go home and get some rest. We'll make certain your grandfather receives the best medical care available today.''

She managed a weak smile. ''Thank you, Dr. Lawrence.'' He nodded, turned and walked away.

''Gus can move into my house,'' Jeremy said close to her ear. ''I already have the hospital bed and a wheelchair.''

Tricia gave him a startled look. ''Where will you sleep?''

''I can sleep on the daybed while you can use an upstairs bedroom. I'll make certain someone will keep Gus's place clean and aired out until he's able to live alone.''

She was puzzled by Jeremy's offer to open his house for her grandfather's convalescence. ''Why are you doing this, Jeremy? You and my grandfather have never been fond of each other.''

''How Gus and I feel about each other is irrelevant, because he is still a member of the farm's extended family. Just like you are,'' he added in a soft tone. ''And you know we always look out for one another.''

Tricia nodded. ''You're right.'' She managed a weak smile. ''Thank you.''

His gaze widened. ''There's no need to thank me. I would do the same for anyone at Blackstone Farms.''

Tricia did not know why, but at that moment she did not want Jeremy to offer his home to Gus just because the elderly man had been a long-time em-

ployee of Blackstone Farms. She wanted it to be because he still felt something for her beyond their
sleeping together.

She had promised to give him the next three weeks
when in reality she wanted it to be the rest of her life.
The harder she had tried to ignore the truth the more
it nagged at her, for it had taken only one night of
passionate lovemaking to conclude that she still loved
Jeremy and would love him for the rest of her life.

Sheldon walked into the waiting room as silently
as a large cat. He stopped, watching the interaction
between his son and Tricia. Clearing his throat, he
moved closer as Tricia and Jeremy sprang apart. "If
there's anything you need me to do for you and Gus,
just ask, Tricia."

Tricia smiled at Sheldon. "Thank you, but Jeremy
has offered to let Grandpa stay in his house until he's
able to live alone again."

Sheldon lifted an eyebrow, stared at his son and
wondered if Jeremy and Tricia had made other plans
that perhaps he should know about. Maybe, just
maybe, he would be given the opportunity to retire,
gain another daughter-in-law and, if he was lucky,
another grandchild.

His gaze shifted to Tricia. "Never forget that
you're family, Tricia. Everyone connected to the farm
is family." He lifted the cardboard container cradling
three foam cups. "Let's go somewhere and get some

coffee that doesn't come out of a vending machine looking like mud.''

Turning, Sheldon led the way out of the hospital, Tricia and Jeremy following.

"Why don't we finish this some other time?"

Sheldon's voice broke into Jeremy's thoughts, his sharp tone filled with annoyance. "No, Pop," he countered. "Let's get it over with now. My recommendation is that you sign for a short-term, high-interest loan to ease your cash flow. Once you sell the mares you can pay it off interest free.''

Sheldon nodded. "In other words I would use or borrow the bank's money at no cost to me.''

"Exactly,'' Jeremy concurred, smiling. "Borrow a little extra because you may see some stock you hadn't planned on buying.''

"Now you sound like Ryan.''

"I'm not into horses like you and Ryan, but I do know horse farms need an infusion of new bloodlines every three to five years. And what Blackstone Farms needs is a three-year-old who will be eligible for next year's Kentucky Derby.''

Nodding in agreement, Sheldon closed the ledger, pushed it aside and watched his son massage his forehead with his fingertips. "Do you still have headaches?''

Jeremy lowered his hand. "They come and go.''

"Do you want me to go back to your place for your medication?''

"No. I've stopped taking it."

"Why?"

"Because I don't like not being in control of what I do or say."

Sheldon gave him a long, penetrating look. "You can tell me it's none of my business but—"

"But you're going to say it anyway," Jeremy countered, smiling.

A rare smile deepened the lines around Sheldon's eyes. "Yes, I am going to say it anyway." He sobered quickly. "What's going on between you and Tricia?"

Jeremy did not move, not even his eyes. "There's nothing going on?" Nothing except that they were lovers once again.

"Do you love her?"

"I'll guess I've always loved her."

"Have you told her how you feel?"

"No."

"Why not?"

Jeremy shrugged a shoulder as he continued to massage his forehead. "We've been apart for too long. I've changed and she's changed. If we had re-connected ten years ago or even last year, then I believe things would be different."

"Why would you say that?" Sheldon asked.

"Look at me, Pop. Whenever I have the flashbacks, I feel as if I'm losing my mind. Tricia remembers me whole and sane, not crippled and crazy."

Sheldon leaned forward. "You're not a cripple."

"Get real, Pop. The doctor says I'm healing nicely,

but he knows and I know that I'm through with undercover assignments.''

"I'm going to be honest when I say I'm not sorry about that.''

"That's because you never supported my career choice.''

"You belong here, Jeremy. You should've come back after you graduated from college.''

"I couldn't come back.''

"Why not?''

Sheldon sat silently as Jeremy repeated what Russell Smith and Gus Parker told him that fateful night fourteen years before. "I've spent years beating myself up for breaking up with Tricia. I wanted to hate her, but every time I came back to the farm I prayed she'd be here.''

"Has she forgiven you?''

A smile inched its way through the uncertain expression on Jeremy's lean face. "As much as she can, given the circumstances. Before Gus's heart attack she said she'd give me three weeks.''

"Is that what she said?''

Jeremy nodded. "Loud and clear.''

Sheldon ran a hand over his face. "Damn. She's as stubborn as Gus,'' he drawled. He angled his head. "I stopped dispensing fatherly advice after you and Ryan became men, but there comes a time when it is necessary. Put aside your pride and grovel.''

Jeremy stared at Sheldon, complete surprise on his

face. "I know you're not talking about pleading and begging."

"If it comes to that."

There was a moment of silence before Jeremy's expression hardened noticeably. "Do you want me to patch things up with Tricia because you want to retire?"

Sheldon's eyes darkened like angry clouds as he pushed back his chair and stood up. "My decision to retire is not predicated on your love life." He spat out the word. "So, don't delude yourself, Jeremy. It's just that I've been where you are right now. There were people who did not want me to get together with your mother, but at seventeen I had more of a backbone than you have at thirty-two."

Jeremy's expression was thunderous as he watched his father walk out of the room. What did Sheldon expect him to do? What more could he do? He couldn't force Tricia to remain at the farm if she chose to leave.

More important, he was unable to tell Tricia he still loved her, because he did not want to become that vulnerable again. And given his present emotional state he did not think he would make it back from the brink of madness this time if he offered her his heart only to have her reject him.

However, there was one thing he knew for certain, which was that time was on his side. The longer she stayed the more time they had to regain each other's trust.

* * *

Two days after Gus was wheeled into the intensive care unit, he was transferred to a private room. Although oxygen flowed into his nostrils, an intravenous feeding tube was taped to the back of his right hand and his vitals were closely monitored by the electrodes taped to his chest, he was resting comfortably. His color was ashen, and what was left of his sparse white hair appeared brittle.

Tricia squeezed a dab of moisturizing hair cream into her hand, massaged it gently into his hair and scalp before she combed his hair.

Gus opened his eyes and stared up at Tricia. The last time he remembered seeing her was at the bungalow. The minute lines around his eyes deepened as he managed a tentative smile. "Hey, grandbaby girl."

She leaned over and kissed his cheek. "Hi, Grandpa. How are you feeling this morning?"

"Good." He let out an audible sigh. "I'm sorry if I gave you a scare."

"There's no need to apologize. In fact I was pretty cool," she lied smoothly. There was no way she was going to admit to Gus that she was almost hysterical by the time Ryan came to the bungalow to take him to the hospital. At that moment her medical training fled, leaving in its wake a woman who feared losing her last surviving relative.

There came a light knock on the door. Tricia turned to find Jeremy and Sheldon in the doorway. Sheldon cradled a large bouquet of flowers against his chest.

Her gaze met and fused with Jeremy's. Over the past three days they hadn't seen much of each other. She dropped him off at Sheldon's house in the morning, then drove to the hospital to spend the day with Gus. She returned to the farm at night, picked Jeremy up from his father's house and drove him back home.

They shared a bed but hadn't made love since the night they'd checked into the bed-and-breakfast, and Tricia had come to know a very different Jeremy. Whenever she cried because she feared losing her grandfather, he held her while offering words of comfort and encouragement. She had promised Sheldon that she would take care of his son, but the roles were now reversed because now Jeremy took care of her.

Gus gestured with his left hand. "Come in and sit down."

Sheldon placed the basket of flowers on the window ledge and sat in a chair in the corner, while Jeremy took a chair at the foot of the bed.

Sheldon smiled at Gus. "The flowers are from the folks at the farm." He crossed one knee over the other. "How are you feeling?"

Gus smiled at his friend and former employer. "Pretty good."

"Good enough to hang out with the Wild Bunch for our annual fall camping weekend?" Sheldon and three other men had formed a bond that went beyond employer-employee whenever they went away together. They stayed in a cabin at the foot of the Appalachian Mountains for a male-bonding weekend

that included fishing, marathon poker games, empty-
ing a keg of beer and smoking cigars.

"I'm game, but I don't know if I can smoke cigars
anymore."

Tricia went completely still. "Grandpa!"

Gus stared at his granddaughter. "What's the matter?"

"I didn't know you smoked cigars."

He waved a frail hand. "I only do it once a year."

"Once a year is too much. No more cigars,
Grandpa. I mean it," Tricia added when Gus rolled
his eyes at her.

The elderly man's gaze shifted to Jeremy. "Does
she treat you like this?"

Jeremy nodded. "All the time."

Tricia's jaw dropped. "No, I don't."

"She's even threatened me," he continued as if
Tricia were not in the room.

Gus fixed a steady gaze on Jeremy. "Fourteen
years ago Tricia told me that the two of you planned
to marry after you graduated college."

There was complete silence from the four occu-
pants, while the soft beeping sounds coming from the
machine monitoring Gus's respiration, heartbeat and
blood pressure reverberated in the stillness.

Sheldon leaned forward on his chair, his startled
gaze shifting from Jeremy to Tricia.

Tricia's eyes widened as she held her breath.

Only Jeremy and Gus appeared calm, composed.

"That's true," Jeremy said.

Gus pressed a button, raising the head of his bed. "Come here, son." Jeremy pushed to his feet and approached the bed. Turning his head slowly, Gus stared at Tricia. "Please come here, grandbaby. I want you to stand next to Jeremy." Tricia gave Jeremy a questioning look and rounded the bed.

Gus took a deep breath. "I'm going to say this quickly and be done with it because I'm tired." His gaze was fixed on the ceiling. "Staring death in the face is scary. Olga used to call me a fool, and after all these years I'm forced to agree with her. I interfered with something I should have left alone." Turning his head slowly, he stared at Tricia, then Jeremy. "Jeremy Blackstone, I want you to marry my granddaughter. Marry her, protect her and give me at least one great-grandbaby before I leave this world."

Heat flamed in Tricia's face. "No, Grandpa!"

Gus glared at Tricia. "Hush up. I'm not talking to you." He ignored her slack jaw. "Sheldon, you should be a part of this." Waiting until Sheldon moved closer to the bed, Gus said, "I want you to get someone to help Tricia plan her wedding."

A grim-faced Sheldon folded his arms over his chest. He shook his head slowly. "Sorry, Gus. I don't intend to become a party to coercion or manipulation. If Tricia and Jeremy want to marry, then it must be their decision." He turned to Tricia. "The only thing I'm going to say is that I'd be honored to call you daughter."

Tricia felt like a specimen on a slide under a microscope. The energy radiating from the three men was almost as tangible as the annoyance and anger knotting her insides.

Her dark eyes bore into her grandfather's. "I love you, Grandpa, but I'm not going to allow you to control my life, and I don't need you to speak for me."

Jeremy's expression was a mask of stone. "You don't have to say anything, Tricia. Just because Gus is your grandfather, I will not stand by and let him intimidate you."

Gus reached for the buzzer to the nurses' station. Less than a minute later, a white-clad figure walked into the room. "Yes, Mr. Parker?" the nurse asked.

Gus waved his hand weakly. "Please show these people out."

The nurse folded her hands on her hips. "Gentlemen, madam, I'm going to ask you to leave now."

Tricia could not believe they had been so summarily dismissed. She was hard-pressed not to come back at Gus. "I'll see you later, Grandpa."

Gus averted his head. "Don't come back to see me unless you have a wedding date."

Sheldon patted Gus's shoulder. "Don't push it, friend."

Sheldon followed Jeremy and Tricia out of the room, smiling and shaking his head. He did not agree with Gus's scheme, but if his son did propose to Tricia, then everyone would get what they wanted: Jeremy and Tricia would marry, he would gain another daughter-in-law, and perhaps he and Gus could look forward to a new grandchild and great-grandchild respectively.

Nine

Tricia sat on the chaise between Jeremy's out-stretched legs, staring up at the star-studded sky and struggling to bring her fragile emotions under control.

"Why is he doing this to me? To us?" There was a sob in her voice.

Lowering his head, Jeremy pressed his lips to her hair. "I don't know, sweetheart."

She glanced over her shoulder. Light from porch lamps threw long and short shadows over his face. "My grandfather is shutting me out because I refuse to bend to his will."

Tricia had gone to the hospital to see Gus that afternoon, but he wouldn't talk to her and ordered her out of his room after she told him that she had no intention of marrying Jeremy.

"Gus has always been a proud man."

"My grandfather is living in the wrong century. Shotgun weddings are a thing of the past."

Jeremy traced the outline of her ear with a forefinger. "You should try to see things his way, Tricia. He blames himself because we're not together. I suppose forcing us to marry is his way of trying to right the wrongs."

She shifted and stared directly at the man holding her to his heart. "You agree with him?"

He shook his head slowly. "No, Tricia, I don't agree with him. But I do understand why he'd want you to marry me."

She was caught off guard by the husky quality of his voice. Tricia stared at Jeremy as if he were a stranger. There was only the sound of their measured breathing, the incessant chirping of crickets and an occasional hoot of an owl.

"Why?" she asked once she'd recovered her voice.

"In your grandfather's day, women needed men to protect them. To his way of thinking, as my wife you would be a Virginia Blackstone and under my and my family's protection. I don't have to tell you what that means."

As soon as she had learned to read, Tricia became aware of the significance of the Blackstone name in the annals of horseracing. "You make it sound so simple. You get a wife, I get a husband, and my grandfather is absolved of his guilt."

"It sounds simple because it is simple."

She eased out of his loose embrace and stood up. "Nothing is ever that simple...and it...it's just too late," she said. "Listen Jeremy, I've had about as much as I can take for one day. I'm going to bed. Are you coming?"

He stared up at her. "I'm going to sit out here for a while."

She nodded. "Good night."

Tricia was awakened by the press of a hard body along the length of hers. "Jeremy." His name was a whisper.

"Why are you sleeping down here?" Since Jeremy decided that Gus would convalesce under his roof, he and Tricia had begun sleeping together in the master bedroom. He hoped they would continue to share a bed until her grandfather was discharged from the hospital.

Tricia sat up on the daybed and combed her fingers through her short, curly hair. "I needed to be alone so I could think."

Jeremy reached for her hand. "What is there to think about? You and I are going to be married."

She went completely still, unable to believe what she'd just heard. "What?"

Jeremy gathered her to his chest and rested his chin on the top of her head. "We should've married ten years ago. We have lost so much."

Tricia felt the slow, strong pumping of his heart

against her cheek. "We can't turn back the clock," she argued softly.

He tightened his hold on her body. "Perhaps not, but we can move forward."

He still loved her, had never stopped loving her. The realization had attacked him as he sat on the porch that evening mentally playing back his life like reversing a video. He vacillated between the emotions of self-pity because of his injury and gratitude because his life had been spared, but in his selfishness he had forgotten that he was a son, brother and an uncle. He had a family who loved him as much as he loved them.

And, he had been reunited with a woman he had loved for so long that he could not remember when he did not love her. She had married another man, yet she had not forgotten him. She loved him when he had done nothing to deserve her love. He had run away and deserted her when she needed him.

Anchoring a finger under her chin, he raised her face. The soft glow from the lamp on a side table highlighted a pair of large dark eyes filled with confusion and uncertainty.

"Marry me, Tricia."

She blinked once. "Is this what you want to do?"

Jeremy nodded. "Yes. It is something we should've done ten years ago."

Leaning forward, she rested her forehead against his shoulder and inhaled the lingering scent of his cologne. Jeremy had asked her to marry him, yet there was no mention of the word *love* in his proposal.

She closed her eyes and prayed silently, prayed she would make the right decision. "What is there about me that makes men propose marriage when I'm most vulnerable?"

Jeremy felt her uneasiness. What Tricia did not know was he also was vulnerable, vulnerable to her rejection, vulnerable to the emotional pain only she could inflict.

"Let me take care of you, baby. I promise to protect you from all that is seen and unseen, while providing you with financial security. Gus is the only family you have, but when you marry me, Sheldon will become your father, Ryan your brother, Kelly your sister and Vivienne and Sean your nephew and niece."

Tricia did not want to think of the time when she would lose her last surviving relative. "Can we do this, Jeremy?"

"Yes, we can."

Easing back, she stared up at him. The tenderness shimmering in his smoky-gray gaze took her breath away. A sensual smile softened her mouth. "Okay, Jeremy. Let's do it."

Jeremy angled his head and brushed his mouth over her parted lips. "Thank you, baby, for giving us a second chance. Let's go upstairs. I have to give you something."

* * *

Tricia sat on the bed in the master bedroom, holding her breath as Jeremy slipped a ring with a flawless, square-cut emerald set in a band of pavé diamonds on her finger.

"My father gave this ring to my mother as a gift after Blackstone Farms' first Kentucky Derby winner. Boo-Yaw wasn't favored to come in among the three favored, but he fooled everyone when he won by a nose." Boo-Yaw went on to win many more races for Blackstone Farms, and after he no longer raced competitively, he went on to sire several more champions.

Jeremy had given Tricia a small box filled with priceless heirloom pieces that had once belonged to his mother and grandmother. There was an estate diamond ring that would have made a perfect engagement ring, but she had decided on the emerald because it was her birthstone.

Jeremy kissed her cheek. "It's a perfect fit."

She extended her hand. "It's beautiful."

He nuzzled her ear. "Not as beautiful as you are."

Not only did she feel beautiful, but she also felt complete for the first time in many, many years. She and Jeremy had so much to make up for. Once he had proposed marriage she thought about what she would have to give up and the answer was: not much. She owned property she could sell and now had a profession she could make the most of at Blackstone Farms Day School. She planned to apply for the position of school nurse. She did not have a boyfriend, lover or close girlfriends in Baltimore, and that meant her departure would be accomplished without a lot of fanfare.

Glancing up, she met Jeremy's tender gaze. "We're going to have to select a wedding date."

He rapped his knuckles on the cast. "I'd like to wait until this is off. Repeating my wedding vows leaning on a pair of crutches doesn't quite cut it."

"Then we'll wait," Tricia said softly.

Jeremy lay on his back, his gaze fusing with hers. "How about the Labor Day weekend?"

She gave him a sensual smile. "That will give me enough time to plan something that won't be too elaborate."

"We can marry here on the farm, especially since that's a holiday when everyone gets together." His gaze softened. "There are so many things I want to do with you, but I can't right now."

She crawled over his body, laughing softly. "I promise not to take advantage of you."

He curved his arms around her waist; her breasts spilled over the lacy bodice of her nightgown. "I won't say a word if you decide to use or abuse me as long as it feels good," he said teasingly. A swollen silence ensued before Jeremy said, "I've decided to leave the DEA."

Raising her head, Tricia stared down at him. "Are you certain that is what you want to do?"

Jeremy nodded. "I've been giving it a lot of

thought. I know if I stay in I'd probably be assigned to a desk position, and that would turn me into a certifiable basket case. My first session with the psychiatrist was a complete disaster. He wanted me to talk about what happened to me and the other members of my team before we were rescued and I refused.''

''What are you going to do?''

A slow smile spread over his face. ''Are you concerned that I won't be able to support you?''

Tricia felt her face burn in embarrassment. ''Of course not. It's…'' His fingers stopped her protest.

''I'm going to assume the responsibility of running the farm,'' he said in a quiet tone. ''Pop has been talking about retiring, and Ryan has been on my case for years about taking my rightful place at Blackstone Farms.'' His expression softened. ''If I hadn't broken my ankle none of this would've become a reality. I would not have come back to stay more than two or three days, and I probably would not have reconnected with you.''

Tricia lay motionless and registered the steady pumping of her fiancé's heart under her breasts. His heartbeat was strong while her grandfather's was weak. ''Hold me, Jeremy.''

''I am,'' he said against her ear. Tightening his hold on her body, Jeremy knew this coming together was not about sex. It was about easing Tricia's apprehension about her grandfather's and their future. It was about offering his love and his protection. The fingertips of his right hand made tiny circles along her spine. "I'll always be here for you, darling."

She nodded and placed light kisses along the column of his strong neck, forehead, eyelids, nose, cheekbones, chin and mouth. She paused to remove his clothes, then her rapacious mouth charted a path from his throat to his belly and lower. And she broke her promise not to take advantage of Jeremy as she wrung a passion from him that left him gasping for his next labored breath.

Jeremy threw a muscled arm over his face and groaned in erotic pleasure that was akin to pain. "Please, please, please," he whispered over and over until it became a litany.

Tricia ignored his pleas and loved him for all of the years they'd been apart, and when he finally released his boiling passion she could not disguise her body's reaction as she moved up his chest and gloried in his hardness pulsing against her thighs.

They lay, their arms entwined and waited for the heat to fade. Tricia lay down beside Jeremy and within minutes she had fallen asleep. But sleep was not as kind to Jeremy, although he was filled with an amazing sense of completeness.

It would take time for him to believe that everything he had ever wanted for himself was about to be manifested: the girl he had spent years protecting, the young woman with whom he had fallen in love would become his wife in another month.

* * *

Tricia sat beside Jeremy on a glider on Sheldon's porch, her right hand cradled in his larger left one. They had decided to inform Sheldon of their upcoming nuptials before going to the hospital to visit Gus.

Sheldon's sharp gaze lingered on the emerald and diamond ring on her left hand. A wry smile touched his mouth. "I know Julia would have been pleased to know you are wearing her ring. It was her favorite."

Tricia stared at her outstretched fingers. "I'm honored to be able to wear it."

Sheldon appeared lost in thought as he recalled the exact moment he had given Julia the ring. "When's the big day?"

Tricia stared at Jeremy's distinctive profile. "We've decided on the Labor Day weekend," he said in a deep, quiet tone.

Sheldon smiled. "Excellent choice." Memorial Day, the Fourth of July and Labor Day were Blackstone Farms get-togethers.

"Let me know what you want to serve and I'll have Cook put together a menu for you," Sheldon continued.

Tricia nodded, smiling. "I'm going to ask Kelly to help me with the planning."

Sheldon rose to his feet, leaned over and kissed Tricia's cheek. "Congratulations and welcome to the family."

"Thank you, Sheldon."

He wagged a finger at her. "Now that you're going to become my daughter, I want you to call me Pop."

Her smile was dazzling. "Okay. Thank you, Pop."

Reaching for his crutches, Jeremy pushed to his feet. "We're going to see Gus and give him the good news."

"Tell Gus I'll see him later," Sheldon said as he watched Tricia curve an arm around Jeremy's waist as they left the porch and made their way to Tricia's car.

A rare smile crinkled his eyes as he watched the young couple drive away. He wasn't certain whether it was Gus's manipulation or that Jeremy and Tricia had come to their senses and realized they belonged together, but he was ecstatic about their decision.

His smile widened. Jeremy and Tricia weren't the only ones planning their future. At the end of the year he would officially retire from the day-to-day operation of Blackstone Farms and do a few things he'd put off doing for years.

Tricia found her grandfather in the solarium watching an all-news cable television station. He spied her and Jeremy as soon as they walked in the sun-filled room.

"Hi, Grandpa."

Gus glared at Tricia and Jeremy. "You got something to tell me?"

Jeremy hobbled over to Gus and sat beside him. "I've plenty to tell you, Gus. Tricia and I plan to marry during the Labor Day weekend." He ignored the older man's gasp of surprise. "And I'd be honored if you would give me your granddaughter's hand in marriage.''

Gus's hand shook noticeably as he reached out and touched Jeremy's broad one. "Nothing would make me happier.''

Tricia sat on her grandfather's left and showed him the ring on her finger. Her eyes welled with tears when Gus covered her hand with his, gently squeezing her fingers. Resting her head on his shoulder, she closed her eyes.

"Hurry up and get well, Grandpa.''

"I will, grandbaby girl. Nothing, and I do mean nothing will stop me from attending your wedding.''

Tricia and Jeremy sat with Gus until a technician came to take him back to his room for an EKG. They left the hospital, and instead of returning to the farm, Tricia headed toward Richmond. She needed to shop for a wedding dress.

Ten

Tricia walked into the expanded schoolhouse with Kelly Blackstone, awed by the spaciousness of the newly constructed classrooms. She followed her soon-to-be sister-in-law down a highly waxed hallway to the office she would occupy once the school year began.

Four-week-old Vivienne lay quietly in the carrier held in Kelly's firm grip. The baby seemed fascinated by her toes until she fell asleep during the short drive from her parents' house to the schoolhouse.

The original building, constructed for preschool children, was connected to three one-story buildings that were set up for grades one to three and four to six, and the fourth would house the principal and nurse's office, gymnasium, auditorium, library and cafeteria. The schoolhouse also boasted a square with an interior courtyard playground.

Kelly stopped in front of a door bearing a brass nameplate that read: Mrs. Tricia Blackstone, Nurse. Tricia blushed at her own excitement. It would be another two days before she would marry Jeremy and become Mrs. Blackstone, but seeing it on the door made what was to come more of a reality.

She smiled at Kelly. "It looks very nice."

Kelly returned her smile. "I told the contractor I wanted your door with your nameplate up first." The doors to all the classrooms and offices lay on dollies in the hallways.

Tricia gave Kelly a quick hug. "Thank you."

Ryan's wife had become the sister Tricia never had. Soon after she and Jeremy officially announced their engagement Kelly had thrown all of her energies into helping Tricia with her wedding plans.

Tricia liked Kelly and thought her the perfect partner for Ryan. She was kind, friendly, unpretentious and the complete opposite of the first woman he'd married. Tall and slender with a fashionably cut hairstyle, Kelly had an overabundance of energy she had channeled to become a successful wife, mother and educator.

The two women walked in and out of spaces that were to become classrooms and a science lab. "Will everything be finished before the beginning of classes?" Tricia asked.

Kelly led the way back to the parking lot where she'd parked her SUV. Vans and pickup trucks belonging to the workmen filled up many of the spaces. "The contractor reassures Sheldon that his men will be finished a week before the start of classes. All of the furniture has been sitting in a warehouse in Richmond awaiting word when it should be delivered."

"Have you hired everyone?" Tricia asked after Kelly secured Vivienne in a car seat and sat behind the wheel.

"I still need a librarian." Her gold-brown gaze met Tricia's dark one. "Do you know someone who would be interested in the position?"

"I had a friend when I lived in New York who was studying to become a librarian. I'll have to look through some of my old telephone books to see if I can find her number."

Kelly turned the key in the ignition. "I've placed several ads in some newspapers and contacted placement offices at several colleges."

"You still have time before the school year begins, so maybe you'll get someone."

"I like your optimism, Tricia." She shifted into reverse and backed out of the lot. "I don't know about you, but right about now I'd like some ice cream from Shorty's Diner."

Tricia glanced at her watch. It was after four. "You want to eat ice cream now?"

"Yes, ma'am."

"We don't have to go into town to eat at Shorty's. Cook always has ice cream at the dining hall."

Kelly sucked her teeth. "Cook buys store-bought ice cream. I want homemade."

It was Tricia's turn to suck her teeth. "I've been counting every calorie and gram that has gone into my mouth so that I won't look like a stuffed sausage in my wedding dress, and you want me to eat ice cream." She'd dropped a dress size, going from an eighteen to a sixteen.

Kelly gave her a sidelong glance. "You don't have to eat it. You can hold Vivienne and watch me instead." Crossing her arms under her breasts, Tricia mumbled angrily under her breath about skinny women.

"I don't know whether you're aware of it or not," Kelly continued, deliberately ignoring Tricia's reference to skinny women, "but whenever you walk into a room every man has the potential for whiplash. You are the most beautifully proportioned full-figured woman I've ever seen.

"And don't forget you caused quite a stir last Saturday when you went swimming wearing that red one-piece number. The only guys who didn't hear it from their wives or significant others were the ones who were wearing sunglasses. One of the grooms was staring so hard I'm certain he popped a few blood vessels."

Tricia's dark eyes sparkled as she smiled. "You're good for a girl's ego, Kelly."

"I only speak the truth, girlfriend."

The swimsuit was the most modest one she owned yet Jeremy had asked whether she really intended to wear it. Her answer had been the affirmative, which left him in a funk for days. His bad mood ended once the cast was removed from his left leg.

A smug smile touched Tricia's mouth as she thought about Jeremy and her grandfather. Gus's attitude toward Jeremy softened once he moved into his house. He insisted the younger man call him Grandpa instead of his given name, taught him how to bluff at poker and more about horses than Jeremy had learned in the first eighteen years he'd lived on the horse farm.

Kelly drove to Staunton and parked alongside a restaurant that resembled a 1950s jukebox. Tricia nursed a club soda and watched Kelly eat a vanilla sundae topped with nuts, whipped cream and fresh berries. It was close to six o'clock when they finally got into the sport utility vehicle to return to Blackstone Farms. They were further delayed because Kelly had gone into the restaurant's bathroom to breastfeed Vivienne once the baby woke up crying to be fed.

Kelly maneuvered into a parking space at the dining hall and turned off the engine, while Tricia got out and gathered Vivienne from her safety seat. She was now able to hold the infant without losing her composure. Vivienne looked as much like her mother as Juliet had Jeremy.

"She probably needs to be changed, and I don't have any more diapers with me," Kelly said, as Vivienne woke up fretfully. Tricia handed Kelly her daughter, who returned the baby to the safety seat. "I'm going back to the house. Go on in. I won't be long."

Tricia waited for Kelly to drive away before she made her way to the entrance of the dining hall. She opened the door and went completely still as a roar of *"Surprise!"* greeted her.

Her shocked gaze lingered on Jeremy leaning on a cane, grinning from ear to ear. A large, printed banner reading Congratulations to Tricia and Jeremy! hung from a wall under which a long table overflowed with gaily wrapped gifts. Covering her face with her hands, she squeezed back tears. Now she knew why Kelly delayed coming back to the farm.

Leaning heavily on his cane, Jeremy limped over to Tricia, curved an arm around her waist, lowered his head and covered her mouth with his. Her arms circled his neck and she kissed him back.

"Get a room!" someone shouted. The dining hall erupted in laughter.

"Save some for the wedding night," came another deep voice.

Jeremy ended the kiss and gave Tricia a sensual smile. "I hope someone took a picture of you when you walked in because the look on your face was priceless.''

Tricia rolled her eyes at him. ''I have to assume you were in on this.''

He nodded. ''Guilty as charged. Come sit down and eat before you open your gifts.'' He led her over to the table where Gus sat with Sheldon.

She kissed her grandfather's cheek, then Sheldon's before he pulled out a chair for her. ''How long have you guys been planning this?''

''Actually it was Kelly's idea,'' Sheldon said. ''When she overheard me and Ryan talk about making arrangements for the moving company to pack up your house she said they should catalogue the entire contents including color schemes. She made up a list of things she thought you'd like and set up a wedding registry.''

Tricia stared at Jeremy. ''To say I was clueless is an understatement, because I've never known anyone at Blackstone Farms to keep a secret for more than twenty four hours.''

''I beg to differ with you,'' Sheldon countered. ''I had no idea you and my son were keeping company as kids.''

Jeremy stared at his father. ''We didn't begin, as you say, 'keeping company' until we were eighteen.''

Tricia glanced across the table, meeting her grandfather's solemn gaze. There was no doubt he was thinking about his own daughter, who had dropped out of school and became a mother before she was eighteen.

Tricia's gnawing need to know about the man who had fathered her and the whereabouts of her mother had eased after Gus's heart attack. The fear of losing her grandfather forced her to reexamine herself and those she loved. If Patricia Parker wanted to see her, then she would've made the attempt. After all Patricia had had thirty-two years to reconnect with Tricia.

A waiter approached the table, pen and pad in hand. "Is everyone ready to order?"

Tricia reached for the printout of the dinner choices and perused it as Sheldon, Gus and Jeremy gave the young man their selections. The dining hall's furnishings were reminiscent of upscale New York City restaurants: dark paneled walls with stained-glass insets, plush carpeting, linen-covered tables and Tiffany-style table lamps. Breakfast and lunches were buffet, but dinners were always served. The exceptions were pre- and postrace celebrations. Weather permitting, these functions were held outdoors.

Tricia glanced up at the waiter. "I'll have the Caesar salad with grilled chicken."

She redirected her attention to Jeremy and reached for his hand under the table. He looked nothing like the heavily sedated man she'd been reunited with after more than a decade. He'd gained weight and there was a sprinkling of gray in his close-cropped black hair.

Jeremy shifted his chair closer to Tricia's, silently

admiring her delicate profile. "Do you know how hard it has been not to sneak upstairs and climb into bed with you?"

She lowered her gaze, enchanting him with the demure gesture. "I thought you liked having Grandpa as a roommate." Her voice was as hushed as Jeremy's.

"Believe it or not he's a real cool dude."

Tricia smiled. She'd heard people call Gus a lot of things, but never a "cool dude."

Conversations faded as waiters and waitresses began bringing out dishes from the kitchen for the more than thirty people filling up the dining hall. Gus and Sheldon exchanged a knowing look before Gus pushed back his chair and stood up. A hush fell over the room.

Tricia stared up at the man who was both father and grandfather. He'd managed to put on a little of the weight he'd lost when hospitalized and although still gaunt he appeared elegantly serene.

He cleared his voice and smiled at Tricia. "I'd just like to say a few words before we begin our meal. I have so much to be grateful for—for Tricia being at the right place at the right time when I suffered a heart attack, for her putting up with her cantankerous grandfather and for Jeremy who helped make me aware of the power of forgiveness."

Gus closed his eyes and when he opened them they glistened with unshed moisture. Sheldon rose to his feet and gave the older man a rough embrace as applause filled the space.

Ryan and his family walked into the dining hall and sat at a nearby table. He snapped Vivienne's carrier into the high chair, pushing it under the table. Leaning over, he tapped Jeremy's shoulder. "What did we miss?" he whispered.

"Gus becoming maudlin."

"No!" There was an incredulous look on Ryan's handsome face.

"Believe it, brother."

Tricia hid a smile when she heard the exchange between Jeremy and his brother. She didn't know whether it was Gus's brush with death or her agreeing to marry Jeremy and live at the farm that had changed him, but whatever the catalyst, she hoped the change was permanent.

Tricia felt slightly tipsy from the champagne that had been served with delicate pastries and petit fours prepared for the occasion by the pastry chef. She rose unsteadily to her feet as a few of the farm residents began chanting her name.

Jeremy touched her hand. "Would you like to use my cane, sweetheart?"

She ignored his remark and made her way to the table laden with gifts. She sat on a chair decorated with streamers of white satin.

There was a pregnant hush when she picked up the first package. Decorative paper, ribbon and bows were discarded as she opened boxes containing gourmet cookware, silver and crystal picture frames, exquisite Egyptian cotton linen, plush bath towels, scented candles, hand-painted flowerpots, bathroom accessories, an espresso-cappuccino machine, personalized stationery imprinted with both her and Jeremy's names and an antique soup tureen from Kelly.

When she'd admired the fragile china piece, circa 1850, she'd never thought Kelly would give it to her as a wedding gift. Smiling at Kelly, Tricia mouthed "Thank you very much."

Tricia sat on the floor of the porch between Jeremy's outstretched legs, her elbows resting on his knees. They'd returned from the dining hall, put Gus to bed and then retreated to the porch. The mercury was in the low seventies, the night sky ablaze with summer constellations.

Jeremy leaned forward on the rocker and toyed with the curls on the nape of her neck. "Are you nervous?"

"A little." Tricia's breath was a hushed whisper. "I take that back. I'm frightened, Jeremy."

His fingers stilled. "Why?"

"I keep thinking something is going to happen that will prevent us from getting married."

Leaning down, Jeremy pressed a kiss to her fragrant curls. "Nothing's going to happen, sweetheart. Saturday, at exactly four o'clock you and I are going to stand in front of Judge Campbell and take our vows with our family and friends as witnesses.

"We're going to hang around long enough to share a toast, eat cake, then we are going to disappear for the next three days."

Tilting her chin, Tricia stared up at Jeremy. The soft light from porch lamps flattered his deeply tanned face. His white linen shirt was unbuttoned to his waist, and each time she glanced at his furred chest she found it hard to swallow.

"I feel guilty leaving Grandpa."

"He's going to be all right staying with Pop. He has already made arrangements with a registry to have a nurse come out and check on him."

Tricia nodded. She and Jeremy planned to spend three days at Sheldon's cabin near the West Virginia border. Reaching up, she grasped his hands and squeezed them gently.

"I love you, Jeremy."

There was a pulse beat of silence before he said, "I love you, too."

Her eyes filled with tears, but they didn't fall. It was the first since they were reunited that he admitted to loving her.

Tricia felt as if she was on a runaway roller coaster that had no intention of stopping as she drove to Richmond for the final fitting of her dress. She had chosen a sleeveless, full length, silk-lined, off-white lace sheath dress covered with seed pearls from the scooped neckline to the scalloped hem. A single strand of opera-length pearls, matching earrings, a garland headpiece made with miniature white roses and a pair of wispy lace shoes with sturdy embroidered heels rounded out the former turn-of-the century romantic ensemble. The seamstress made the adjustments and informed Tricia that the dress would be delivered to Blackstone Farms before noon on Saturday. She left the bridal shop for her scheduled appointment at a day spa.

Dusk had descended on the farm when she returned, feeling as good as she looked. Her skin glowed from a European facial, her hands and feet soft and dewy from a hydrating manicure and pedicure and her body supple and relaxed from a full body massage. She'd had her hair cut and styled so it framed her face in feathery curls.

Her pulse quickened when she spied the pale-blue streamers fluttering from the poles of the large white tent set up in a grassy meadow. The blue matched the yards of organza-swathed chairs lined up in precise rows under the tent. A portable stage for a band and dancing was also in place for the reception that would follow the ceremony.

Tricia maneuvered her car into the driveway behind Jeremy's SUV. A day after the orthopedist removed the cast, he began driving again.

She got out of her car and mounted the porch steps. Pausing on the top step, she stared at her fiancé sprawled on the chaise. Moving closer, she leaned down and kissed him.

A slow smile tilted the corners of Jeremy's mouth upward as he straightened and patted the cushioned seat. "Come sit down."

Tricia sat between his legs and pressed her back to his chest. "Where's Grandpa?"

Jeremy kissed her ear. "He went to bed early. He said he wanted to be rested for tomorrow."

Gus had openly expressed his relief once Tricia revealed she did not want a formal wedding. He had worn a tuxedo for his own wedding, swearing he would never look like a penguin again. The wedding party included Ryan as best man, Kelly as matron of honor and their son, Sean, as ring bearer.

Curving an arm around Tricia's waist, Jeremy shifted her effortlessly until she straddled his lap. "You look fantastic." There was no mistaking the awe in his voice.

She smiled demurely. "Thank you. I've decided I'm going to treat myself to a full body massage at least once a month." The hands cupping her hips feathered up her ribs to cradle her breasts and she drew in a sharp breath. Her head fell limply to his solid shoulder. "What are you doing, Jeremy?" she asked in a trembling whisper.

He laughed deep in his throat. "Offering you a sample of my special massage. You have a choice between the basic, all the way up to the deluxe package." His thumbs caressed her breasts in a sweeping back and forth motion, bringing the nipples into prominence.

Gasping, she breathed heavily against his ear. "What are you charging for the basic package?"

Jeremy's fingers stilled. "The rest of your life."

Easing back in his embrace, Tricia studied his features in the encroaching darkness. "How about the deluxe package?"

"The rest of your life."

Tricia ran a finger down the length of his nose. "You should be reported for price fix—"

Her statement died on her lips when his mouth covered hers in an explosive kiss that sucked the breath from her lungs. She melted into Jeremy's strength, loving him with all of her senses.

They'd promised each other that they wouldn't make love until they were married, but each time he touched her, kissed her, silent screams of unexploded passion roiled with nowhere to escape. Nothing had changed. All Jeremy had to do was fix his smoldering smoky gaze on her, touch her, kiss her and she dissolved into a trembling, heated mass of wanting.

Her lips parted to his probing tongue as she drew it into her mouth. In that instant everything about Jeremy seeped into her and made them one—indivisible. It had been that way the first time they'd become lovers. It hadn't been planned, nothing said, but both had known it was time their friendship had to change. There had been too much awareness of the other, too much sexual tension between them.

Tricia moaned softly when she felt Jeremy's sex hardening under her bottom. She tore her mouth away from his, her smile as intimate as the kiss they'd shared.

"What are you trying to do, seduce me?"

He nodded and offered her a grin that was irresistibly devastating. "I don't plan to go all the way. Just a little kiss here." He pressed his mouth to the area under her ear. "And one here." His voice had lowered seductively as he moved to the fluttering pulse in her throat. "And a little feel here." He gathered the flowing fabric of her dress and slipped his hand under the silken material of her bikini panties.

A shudder shook Tricia. "I think we'd better stop and continue this tomorrow. Same time, different place."

Jeremy released her hip and reached around his back. "I bought you a little something as a wedding gift." She stared at a small square package wrapped in silver paper and tied with velvet ribbon. "Take it, Tricia."

She took it, slipped off the ribbon and peeled away the paper. As soon as she saw the black velvet box she knew it contained a piece of jewelry. She opened the box and went still. Jeremy had given her an exquisite filigree bar pin with a sprinkling of diamonds surrounding a brilliant blue topaz.

Her eyes filled with moisture and she blinked it back before the tears fell. "It's beautiful."

Cupping her chin, he raised her face. "You're

beautiful. I gave you my mother's and grandmother's jewelry, but I wanted you to have something from me that no other woman wore before.''

Curving her arms around his neck, she breathed a kiss under his ear. ''Thank you. I have something for you. Do you want it now or tomorrow?''

''Give it to me tomorrow.''

Tricia dropped her arms and slipped off his lap. ''I'm going upstairs to turn in early. No one wants to see a bride with bags under her eyes.''

Reaching for his cane, Jeremy propelled himself off the chaise. ''I'm going in, too.''

She held the door open for him and they walked through the entryway and into the living room. Corrugated boxes labeled Living Room were stacked in a corner near the curving staircase.

''They were delivered while you were out,'' Jeremy explained.

Tricia nodded. Her future father-in-law had arranged for her furniture to be stored in a warehouse in Richmond until she decided what she wanted to use or give away.

''I'm not going to open one box until after we get back.''

''You don't have to put everything away in one day.''

''I'd like to have them done before the school year begins.''

''Tricia, baby, you have the rest of your life to decorate the house however you wish.''

She knew he was right, but there were changes she wanted to make in the overtly masculine home. "You're right." She kissed his cheek. "Good night."

Jeremy's lids came down, shielding his gaze. "Good night." He watched Tricia walk up the staircase, knowing he would not see her again until she was to become his wife. He planned to rise early and go to his father's house. He, Sheldon, Ryan and Sean would leave together, while Kelly would accompany Tricia and Gus.

He'd asked Tricia to hold on to his heart a long time ago, and in less than twenty-four hours he would claim the only woman he had ever loved as his partner for life.

Eleven

It was a picture-perfect day for an outdoor wedding in Virginia's horse country. Tricia rose early, showered and pulled on a pair of shorts and a T-shirt. Gus was up when she went downstairs, and she decided to prepare breakfast for them instead of ordering it from the dining hall.

Gus sat across the table from Tricia in the large kitchen, his gaze fixed on her face. "You've been asking me about your mother for a long time."

Tricia felt her heart lurch. "If what you intend to tell me is going to make me upset, then I don't want to know. Not on my wedding day, Grandpa."

He reached across the table and his large veined hand covered one of hers. "You don't want to know?"

She shook her head. "Not anymore. I don't need to know where my mother is or who my father was, because the only daddy I know is sitting in front of me. And if my mother wanted to find me all she had to do was come back to Blackstone Farms." She chewed her lower lip for several seconds. "I don't hate my mother, but in all honesty I can't say that I love her because I don't know her. And if she couldn't take care of me, then she did the next best thing giving me to you and Grandma. If I ever meet her one day, then that's something I will tell her."

Gus smiled and character lines deepened around his dark eyes. "You've made me proud, grandbaby girl."

"Thank you." Tricia returned his smile. "I love you, Grandpa." Gus withdrew his hand, dropped his head and stared down at his plate. It was a full minute before his head came up. Pride and tenderness shimmered in his gaze.

They lingered at the table, reminiscing until the doorbell rang. Tricia glanced up at the clock over the stove. It wasn't quite eight o'clock. She got up and made her way to the door.

A young man stood on the other side, holding up a plastic-covered garment on a hanger. It was her dress. She thanked him and returned to the kitchen.

"Do you want to see my dress?" she asked Gus.

He shook his head. "I don't want to see you in all your finery until I'm ready to give you to your young man. I know," he said quickly when he saw Tricia's expression, "his name is Jeremy. He's nice, Tricia. And he's good for you."

She flashed a wide grin. "I hope so, because he's going to become my husband in less than eight hours."

Kelly buttoned the tiny covered buttons on the back of Tricia's dress, then placed the garland of miniature roses on her head. It was the perfect complement to the vintage-style dress. "Make certain you have something old, something new, something borrowed and something blue."

Tricia admired the pale-blue slip dress caressing the curves of Kelly's slim figure. "The pearls are old, my dress is new and the pin has a blue stone." She had affixed Jeremy's wedding gift to the bodice of her dress.

"What about borrowed?"

Her eyes widened. "I don't have anything borrowed." Lifting the hem of the lacy dress, she crossed the room and opened the door to a massive armoire. She pulled out a drawer filled with handkerchief squares and took one. "This will have to do." She refolded the handkerchief, pushing it between her breasts.

Kelly laughed. "There was a time when I used to fill my bra with socks and tissues to make me look bigger. Thanks to Vivienne I no longer need a Wonderbra."

Tricia wanted to tell Kelly that her own breasts had

increased during her pregnancy and breastfeeding, but hadn't returned to their former size. She hadn't begun weaning Juliet when she lost her.

A clock on the mantel of the fireplace chimed the quarter hour. It was 3:45. Waiting until Tricia pulled on a pair of lace gloves, Kelly picked up a bouquet of a combination of creamy-toned roses, hyacinths and astilbe and handed it to her. The stems were wrapped in a long piece of wide white silk ribbon and tied in a bow at the neck of the bouquet. A blue pearl stickpin at the center of the bow held it in place.

"Are you ready, girlfriend?"

Large near-black eyes sparkled like polished onyx. "Yes." The single word mirrored the confidence flowing through Tricia. She had waited a long time for this day.

Kelly pushed her hands into a pair of lace ice-blue gloves, grasped a bouquet made up of blue and white flowers and walked out of the bedroom, Tricia following. They descended the staircase and found Gus, resplendent in a dark-gray suit waiting for them. His smile spoke volumes.

He extended his arm to Tricia. "You look beautiful, grandbaby girl."

Resting her head on his shoulder, Tricia smiled. "Thank you, Grandpa."

Gus covered the gloved hand on his jacket sleeve. "The car is waiting for us." He led her out of Jeremy's house that would soon become Jeremy and Tricia's home to the chauffeur-driven limousine parked in the driveway. The driver assisted Tricia, Gus and then Kelly into the car.

Tricia forced herself not to chew her lower lip and eat away the lipstick the cosmetologist had applied earlier. She closed her eyes and took in deep breaths in an attempt to slow down her runaway pulse. All too soon the ride ended. She opened her eyes and under the tent were rows of chairs occupied by full-time, part-time and resident employees of Blackstone Farms and several neighboring horse farms. At the opposite end of a white carpet littered with white and blue flower petals Jeremy waited with Judge Campbell, Ryan and Sean.

The driver opened the rear door, extending his hand to Kelly. Gus followed and held out his hand to Tricia. She placed hers trustingly in his, smiling.

"Are you ready, Grandpa?"

He raised an eyebrow. "Are you ready, grand-baby?"

She inhaled, then let out her breath slowly. "Yes."

All heads turned to stare at Tricia and Gus when a keyboard player began to play the familiar chords of the wedding march. Kelly led the procession over the carpet, and less than a minute later Gus escorted Tricia over the flower-strewn path to where Jeremy stood, a stunned expression freezing his handsome features.

Jeremy did not want to believe that Tricia could look so innocent and wanton at the same time. The lace skimming her curvy body made her appear ethereal in the streams of diffused sunlight coming into the large tent.

Don't lose it, he told himself over and over as she drew closer. He, who had lost count of the number of times he'd been in situations where his life hung in the balance, was unnerved by the image of a woman he'd loved for so long that he could not remember when he did not love her.

She was now close enough for him to detect the dewy sheen on her flawless face, the scent of the flowers in her bouquet and the soft sensual smell of her perfume.

The judge squared his shoulders under his black robe. "Who gives this woman in marriage?"

"I do." Gus's voice carried easily in the warm air. He took Tricia's hand and placed it in Jeremy's. "Be happy," he whispered before he stepped back and sat down in the chair that had been left vacant for him. He looked across the aisle at Sheldon and smiled.

Sheldon nodded and mouthed, "Boo-yaw!"

Grinning, Gus pumped his fist in the air. He and Sheldon had begun their association as employer and employee, but since his retirement Gus counted Sheldon as a friend and now, with his granddaughter's marriage to Jeremy, family.

"We are gathered together in the sight of God and man to reunite two families in matrimony." Judge Campbell's sonorous voice captured everyone's attention.

Tricia barely registered the judge's words as she stared up into the sooty eyes staring down at her. Jeremy was incredibly handsome in a charcoal-gray pinstriped suit, white shirt and robin's-egg-blue silk tie. His close-cropped raven hair lay neatly on his well-shaped head.

When it came time to exchange vows and rings, she smiled at Sean who stood ramrod straight holding a white pillow with the wedding bands secured with silk ribbon. She handed her bouquet and gloves to Kelly before Jeremy repeated his vows and slipped a band on her hand. Her voice was steady but her hands were shaking when she repeated the gesture.

She heard the judge telling Jeremy he could kiss his bride, and she knew then it was over. Her wish had been granted. She'd waited fourteen years to become Tricia Blackstone.

Her smile was dazzling as she and Jeremy followed Sean, Ryan and Kelly down the carpet to receive the best wishes of those who had come to witness the joining of another generation of Virginia Blackstones.

Tricia curved her arm around her husband's waist inside his suit jacket to steady him. "Careful, hotshot," she teased softly. "Cut another step like that and you'll be on your face."

Jeremy swung her around. "What I want to do is cut out of here."

They had planned to leave right after cutting the cake, but Sheldon offered a toast, a toast that was echoed individually by every farm employee. Teenagers and the young children who now knew that Tricia would become their school nurse offered their own reticent toasts.

"Do you think it's safe to leave now?"

Jeremy glanced over Tricia's head. He met his father's gaze and smiled. He released his wife's hand long enough to pantomime a wave. Sheldon nodded and returned the wave.

"Let's go," Jeremy whispered, leading her out of the tent. They skirted several couples and managed to make it to an area where he had parked his SUV. Their luggage had been loaded in the cargo area earlier that morning.

"How's the ankle holding up?" she asked once Jeremy removed his jacket and sat behind the wheel.

He gave her a quick glance. "It's okay."

"Do you want me to drive?"

"No. I can make it. Sit back and relax, Mrs. Blackstone. I don't want you to plead a headache or fatigue later."

Tricia folded a hand on her hip. "Have you ever known me to plead a headache, Mr. Blackstone?"

Jeremy turned the key in the ignition and shifted into gear. "Nope," he said after a lengthy silence.

Tricia did as Jeremy suggested and closed her eyes. She hadn't realized she had fallen asleep until he shook her gently. "Wake up, sweetheart. We're here."

The house in the mountains was larger than she had

expected. Rising two stories in height, it looked more like a chalet than a rustic cabin. It was surrounded by towering pine trees growing so close together that she doubted whether light reached the earth even during the daylight hours.

Jeremy touched her shoulder. ''I'll be right back.''

Tricia watched as Jeremy made his way to the front door. He hadn't used his cane, and his gait was off. He was scheduled to begin intensive physical therapy the following week, and she hoped the exercise would strengthen his ankle so he would not be left with a limp.

Within minutes golden light blazed from every window so like the many jack-o'-lanterns on display at Blackstone Farms during its annual Halloween celebration.

Jeremy returned, unloaded their luggage and minutes later Tricia found herself in the middle of a large bedroom with an adjoining bath that resembled a European spa with a massive sunken tub with enough room for four people, a free-standing shower and a steam room.

She shivered slightly as warm breath feathered over her nape. Smiling, she said, ''So this is where the Wild Bunch rough it.''

Curving his arms around Tricia's waist, Jeremy lowered his head and trailed kisses along the column of her long neck. ''It's not so rough, is it?''

She rested her hands over the dark-brown ones pressed against her belly. ''I see why they like to come here and hang out. It's better than those over-priced spas in California and Arizona.''

''Will you share a bath with me?''

Tricia closed her eyes. ''Yes.''

Turning her in his embrace, Jeremy cradled her face between his palms. ''I love you so much, Tricia.'' His voice was pregnant with emotion. Her lids fluttered wildly before she met his heated gaze.

''I have to give you your wedding gift.''

A hint of a smile touched Jeremy's mouth. ''You are my wedding, birthday, Christmas, New Year's and every day and holiday gift. I don't need anything—only you.''

Leaning into him, Tricia's lips brushed against his. ''And you're all I'll ever need, Jeremy.'' She kissed him again, then turned in his embrace and presented him with her back. ''Please unbutton me.''

Jeremy made a big production of undoing the little buttons. With each inch of flesh he bared he kissed. The top of the dress slid off her shoulders and the handkerchief fell to the floor. He bent over and picked it up. Tricia quickly explained the significance of something borrowed, eliciting a laugh from him.

''I thought you wanted to plump up your—''

''Don't even go there, Jeremy Blackstone,'' she said, cutting him off. ''I have enough, thank you.''

Slipping his fingers under the straps of her slip, he eased it off her shoulders before unhooking her bra and baring her chest. Her breasts were large and firm like ripened fruit, fruit he wanted to suckle, fruit he wanted to feast on.

Tricia felt the heat of her husband's gaze on her chest, and the area between her legs responded immediately with a rush of moisture that left the nether region pulsing with a need that only Jeremy could assuage.

Jeremy's eyes widened until the dark centers fused with the sooty gray. His nostrils flared as he detected the scent of Tricia's rising desire. She was ready for him.

"I'll be right back." Turning on his heel, he walked stiffly out of the bathroom. He had to get away from Tricia before he ripped the clothes from her body and took her on the tiled floor. He wanted her just that much.

But this was their wedding night, a night in which their coming together would be special enough for them to talk about when they were too old to do more than kiss and hold hands.

Tricia filled the large tub, undressed, hanging up her clothes in a corner closet and opened her vanity case. She'd managed to brush her teeth and cleanse the makeup from her face before Jeremy returned.

He was naked, and recessed lighting shimmered over a tall, lean dark body that reminded her of an African totem representing fertility.

Jeremy pushed a knob on the tub and water pulsed from the many jets. Smiling, he reached for her hand

and led her down four marble steps into the swirling water. Warm water lapped over Tricia's breasts as she floated buoyantly until her toes touched the bottom of the concave tub.

Curving her arms around her husband's strong neck, she kissed him deeply, her tongue curling with his, the scent of mint wafting in her nostrils from his toothpaste and mouthwash.

It had been too long—weeks since they'd made love and Tricia responded like a cat in heat. Her hands swept over his shoulders, chest, breasts, belly and still lower to the hardness bobbing against her inner thigh.

Jeremy threw back his head and groaned loudly. The touch of Tricia's hand squeezing his flesh was like a heated branding iron. He had wanted this coming together to be slow and leisurely, but knew it was not to be. Moving back to a depression built into the tub, he sat, bringing Tricia with him as she straddled his thighs.

Wrapping an arm around her waist, he lifted her easily and she guided his sex into her body. They sighed in unison as flesh closed around flesh.

Bracing his back against the marble ledge, Jeremy watched desire darken Tricia's eyes and face. Cupping her breasts he lowered his head and suckled her, nipples and areolae hardening like tiny pebbles. She met each of his powerful thrusts, giving and receiving in kind.

The passion he had withheld from every woman he had ever known he surrendered to Tricia.

The love he was unable to give any other woman he had ever met he surrendered to Tricia.

The children he'd hoped to have but never risked creating with any woman he surrendered to Tricia.

Everything he was and hoped to be he surrendered to the woman in his arms: his wife.

Tricia melted against Jeremy and her body and world was filled with him. Nothing mattered. The pain and loss of Juliet faded as she lowered her head to Jeremy's shoulder and prayed for the beginnings of new life in her womb.

The pain, hurt, lies and deceit faded completely as a desire she had never known gripped her mind and body, setting them on fire. Her husband became flesh of her flesh, heart of her heart and soul of her soul.

She breathed in deep soul-wrenching drafts as waves of ecstasy throbbed through her lower body. Her hips quickened, moving against Jeremy's in an age-old rhythm that sent scalding blood through her veins.

She was on fire!

Tricia's eager response matched Jeremy's. He felt his flesh hardening, swelling until a familiar sensation signaled their passionate lovemaking was nearing its climax.

He closed his eyes, threw back his head and growled deep in his throat when her pulsing flesh squeezed him tightly. His breath came in long, surrendering moans at the same time Tricia's fingernails bit into the flesh over his shoulders. He welcomed the pain as he succumbed to *le petit mort*. He had faced death again, but this time it was in the most exquisite way possible. It was in the scented embrace of a woman he would love forever.

A moan of ecstasy slipped through Tricia's clenched teeth. She had wanted it to last longer but her body's dormant sexuality was starved for a desire long denied, and she was hurtled beyond the point of no return as a lingering pulsing passion burned like smoldering embers. She clung to Jeremy like a drowning swimmer, her head resting on his shoulder while she waited for her pulse to return to normal.

She closed her eyes and smiled. "I love you," she whispered hoarsely.

Jeremy tightened his grip on her waist. "Love you back."

Tricia and Jeremy returned to Blackstone Farms enveloped in a glow of love and contentment that was obvious to all who glimpsed them. They had spent three days cloistered in the cabin, making love, cooking and planning their future.

Jeremy maneuvered into the driveway to Sheldon's house and cut off the ignition. Shifting, he smiled at Tricia. He had wanted to take her home, but she insisted they stop to see Gus.

Resting his right arm over the back of her seat, he

leaned over and brushed a light kiss over her parted lips. "You're still glowing."

Tricia nuzzled his neck. "That comes from being in love." She had lost count of the number of times they'd made love with each other. It was as if they were insatiable and wanted to make up for the time they were apart. And each time she opened her arms and legs to her husband she opened her heart to accept all Jeremy offered.

Jeremy stepped out of the vehicle to assist Tricia when he spied the familiar figure of his father sitting out on the porch. He waved to the older man.

"Hey, Pop."

Sheldon pushed off the chair and came down the porch. A warm smile softened his sharp features. "Hey, yourself." He offered Jeremy a rough embrace before he leaned into the open passenger-side window and pressed a kiss to Tricia's cheek. "You look wonderful."

Tricia returned his rare smile. "I feel wonderful. We came by to check on my grandfather."

"Gus went out."

"Out!" Tricia practically shouted.

"He went to the movies," Sheldon said quickly. "His nurse thought he would do better if he didn't stay home so much, so she took him to the movies to see a romantic comedy about two middle-aged couples who find love after they join a group for widows and widowers."

Jeremy leaned against the bumper of the SUV and

crossed his arms over his chest. "You should've gone with them. You could use a few pointers about getting back into the dating scene."

Sheldon's eyebrows drew together in a scowl. "Tricia, please take your husband home." Turning on his heel, he mounted the porch stairs and went into the large white house.

Tricia knew Ryan wanted his father to remarry, but this was the first time she'd heard Jeremy mention it. "Jeremy, let's go home."

Jeremy shifted and rested his arm over Tricia's hip. "Do you think I pissed Pop off?"

Tricia opened her eyes and stared out at the shadowy darkness. "You know your father better than I would ever know him, but I suspect he resented your intrusion into his personal life."

"Pop has been alone for too long."

Tricia turned and faced her husband. "He's single by choice, darling. Your father is a very handsome man whom many women would find attractive and consider a very good catch. Once he meets the right woman he'll want to change his marital status without his sons insisting they know what's best for him."

Jeremy's arm tightened on her waist, bringing her body flush against his. "Are you telling me to mind my business?"

She smiled in the dimness of the bedroom. "Yes, my love. No, Jeremy!" she gasped when a hand reached down and covered her feminine heat.

Her protests were short-lived once she found herself sprawled over her husband's chest, and the only
thing that mattered was that she loved the man in her
arms as much as he loved her.

Twelve

Tricia sat on the floor in the living room opening cartons. It had taken her two days to empty the boxes containing items for the kitchen and put everything she intended to keep away. Another day was spent unpacking china, silver and stemware that had once graced her dining room. She preferred her own dining room furniture to the style that Jeremy had selected. When she told him she wanted to make the switch he told her that the house was hers to change, decorate or renovate.

He had begun the responsibility of taking over the reins of running the horse farm from Sheldon. Jeremy, Sheldon and Ryan had established a ritual of meeting after breakfast to discuss the farm's finances and the projected sale of existing stock to increase cash flow. Expanding Blackstone Farms Day School from pre-school to sixth grade had strained the farm's cash reserves. It would take more than two years of tuition from the non-farm students to recoup the expenditures.

Tricia glanced up when she heard familiar footsteps. Jeremy stood over her, smiling. He tightened the knot to a wine-colored tie under the collar of a stark-white shirt. Her wedding gift to him of a pair of white-gold and onyx cufflinks were fitted into the shirt's French cuffs. He and Sheldon were scheduled to go into Richmond for a breakfast meeting with a banker to apply for a short-term loan.

"I have some money," she said without preamble.

Jeremy's hands stilled. "What are you talking about?"

"I have some money," she repeated, "you could use to ease the farm's cash flow." The first time Jeremy discussed the farm's finances with her she thought about the money sitting in a Baltimore bank collecting interest. The money she had received as a settlement and the proceeds from the sale of her home was more than the amount Sheldon intended to borrow.

Jeremy eased his tall frame down to the sofa, his gaze fixed on an open box. Resting atop a sheet of bubble wrap was a photograph of Tricia cradling a baby. At that moment he was grateful he was seated, realizing he could have fallen and reinjured his ankle.

Tricia looked the way she had before she'd left the farm. Her hair was long, and instead of the single braid it flowed around her shoulders in curly ringlets. The child staring out at the camera was an exact replica of the images in his own baby photographs.

She had had his child and not told him!

Rage swelled not permitting him to breathe. "Why didn't you tell me?" The question was squeezed out between his clenched teeth.

"What are—" The words died on Tricia's lips when she noticed the direction of Jeremy's gaze. Sitting atop the box she'd just opened was the only photograph of her with her daughter she'd kept. In her grief, she had cut up all of the others before realizing she would want one tangible memory of her beautiful baby.

She reached out to touch Jeremy's knee, but he jerked away as if she were carrying a communicable disease. Rising to his feet, he glared at her. "Don't touch me."

Tricia went to her knees, her eyes filling with tears. "Jeremy, please. Let me explain."

His hands curled into tight fists as he glowered at the woman he wanted to hate. He shook his head. "No, Tricia. I don't…I can't. Not now."

The tears filling her eyes fell, streaking her face, and she collapsed to the floor not seeing her husband when he walked out of the room. However, she did hear the front door he'd slammed so violently that windows shook. She cried until spent, and when Gus found her she was still on the floor.

He managed to convince her to get off the floor and sit on the sofa. Curving an arm around her shoulders, he pressed a kiss to her short hair. "What's the matter, grandbaby girl?"

Tricia told her grandfather about Jeremy seeing the photograph of her and Juliet. "He hates me, Grandpa."

Gus patted her back. "No, he doesn't. He's hurt because you didn't tell him that he had become a father."

"I have to make him understand that I didn't deliberately deceive him."

"Jeremy loves you, Tricia. And because he does he'll come around."

She wanted to believe her grandfather, but the look on Jeremy's face and his "Don't touch me," said otherwise. Easing out of Gus's protective embrace, Tricia stood up and headed toward the door.

"I'm going out."

Lines of concern creased Gus's forehead. "Are you going to be all right?"

She stopped, not turning, and flashed a wry smile. "Yes. I'm going to wait for my husband to come home, then I'm going to tell him about his daughter."

"You can tell Jeremy about Juliet after I tell you about Patricia and your father." Gus saw Tricia's back stiffened, but she did not move. "Your mother got a part-time job at Sheffield's Hardware the year she turned sixteen. Olga warned her about Sheffield's son, who did not have the best reputation with young women. Patricia wouldn't listen and snuck out nights to meet him.

"Patricia thought he was going to marry her once she told him she was carrying his baby. Of course that never happened because his father had made plans for him to go away to college. She dropped out of school, had you and took up with him again. It all ended after Morgan Sheffield left Staunton to attend college. You were a year old when Patricia put you in my arms and asked me to take care of you. The next time I saw my only child was three months later when I had to go to Tennessee to identify her body. The police told me she'd died of malnutrition. It was apparent she had starved herself to death. I brought her body back and had her cremated.

"I know your pain, grandbaby, because I know how it feels to lose a child. Raising you offered me another chance at parenthood. But once I realized you were involved with Sheldon's son it was like déjà vu. The difference was that Jeremy loved you and he still loves you."

Her shoulders slumping, Tricia nodded. "Thank you, Grandpa, for telling me about my mother. Now I have closure."

She walked out of the house and made her way toward the road that would take her to the north end of the horse farm. A sad smile touched her mouth.

The Sheffields had abandoned their business more than ten years ago, after a Home Depot was erected in a strip mall several miles off the interstate.

Her past behind her, Tricia knew she had to right her future.

The first person Jeremy saw when he returned home after his meeting with the bank president was his wife's grandfather. "Good afternoon, Grandpa."

It actually wasn't a good afternoon because he hadn't been able to concentrate on anything since seeing the photograph of Tricia with his child. The image of the baby with black curly hair and large gray eyes would haunt him to the grave.

Gus nodded, his expression impassive. "Good afternoon, son." He gestured to a nearby chair. "Come, sit down."

"If you don't mind I'd like to talk to Tricia."

"Tricia's not here. Sit down."

Jeremy went completely still. "What do you mean she's not here?"

Gus saw naked fear on Jeremy's face. "She didn't run away, if that's what you're thinking."

"Where is she?"

"She went for a walk."

Turning on his heel, Jeremy retraced his steps off the porch. "I'll see you later."

Gus nodded, watching the tall figure as he walked to his vehicle and drove away. It was obvious Tricia was not her mother because she had fallen in love with a man who loved her unconditionally.

Jeremy let out his breath in a ragged shudder as he stopped and cut off the engine. She was there, sitting under a weeping willow tree, her bare feet in a narrow stream. He had driven to the section of the farm where they'd once picnicked and made love. He walked over to where she sat staring up at him. Her gaze was unwavering as she rose fluidly from the grass.

"If you want a divorce, then I won't contest it."

Jeremy moved closer until they were only inches apart and slipped his hands into the pockets of his trousers to keep from touching his wife.

"There will not be a divorce, Tricia. Not now, not ever. Unless…"

Her eyelids fluttered. "Unless what?"

"You're ready to give me back my heart."

Tricia stared at the man with the luminous eyes that had the power to reach inside her and hold her heart captive. "No, Jeremy. I can't give it back because I don't want to."

A smile softened his mouth. "And I don't want you to." He pulled his hands from his pockets and reached for her. Burying his face in her hair, Jeremy pressed a kiss there. "I can't believe I did the same thing I did fourteen years ago—walk away from you rather than staying to face the truth."

Clinging to her husband, Tricia told Jeremy everything from the moment her pregnancy was confirmed to when she placed a single red rose on the tiny white casket before it lowered into a grave and her subsequent decision to marry Dwight.

"If I had come back to the farm, she never would have died."

Jeremy placed his fingers over her mouth. "Maybe all she was given was three months, darling. She's an angel now." His mouth replaced his fingers and he kissed her. "Our little angel."

Tricia clung to Jeremy, feeding on his strength. "I love you so much."

He smiled. "Love you more."

"I don't think so," she countered.

"Would you like to place a wager, Mrs. Blackstone?"

Easing back, Tricia smiled up at him. "What would I have to wager, Mr. Blackstone?"

"Your heart."

She felt a warm glow flow through her. "I accept, but only if you're willing to wager the same."

"You have it, Tricia. I gave it to you a long time ago."

"How long ago?"

"The first time I peered through the bars of my crib to see you staring back at me."

Leaning back in his embrace, Tricia tilted her head and laughed uncontrollably. Jeremy's laughter joined hers and they were still laughing when they walked into their home and smiled at Gus, who watched them climb the staircase to the second floor.

Jeremy lowered his wife to the bed with the intent of reconciling in the most intimate way possible. They took their time loving each other with all of their senses.

Sated, limbs entwined, hearts beating in unison, Tricia and Jeremy were filled with the peace that had surrounded them from the moment they'd acknowledged their love for each other. It had taken a long time, but they were now ready to plan for another generation of Blackstones.

* * * * *

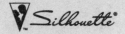

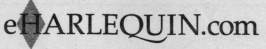

COMING NEXT MONTH

#1615 TERMS OF SURRENDER—Shirley Rogers
Dynasties: The Danforths
When Victoria Danforth and rebellious David Taylor were forced into close quarters on the Taylor plantation, former feuds turned into fiery passion. But unbeknownst to all, Victoria was no farmhand—she was the long-lost Danforth heiress! Could such a discovery put an end to their plantation paradise?

#1616 SINS OF A TANNER—Peggy Moreland
The Tanners of Texas
Melissa Jacobs dreaded asking her ex-lover Whit Taylor for help, but when the smashingly sexy rancher came to her aid, hours spent at her home turned into hours of intimacy. Yet Melissa was hiding a *sinful* secret that could either tear them apart, or bring them together forever.

#1617 FOR SERVICES RENDERED—Anne Marie Winston
Mantalk
When former U.S. Navy SEAL Sam Deering started his own personal protection company, the beautiful Delilah Smith was his first hire. Business relations turned private when Sam offered to change her virgin status. Could the services he rendered turn into more than just a short-term deal?

#1618 SHEIKH'S CASTAWAY—Alexandra Sellers
Sons of the Desert
Princess Noor Ashkani called off her wedding with Sheikh Bari al Khalid when she discovered that his marriage motives did not include the hot passion she so desired. Then a plane crash landed them in the center of an island paradise, turning his faux proposal into unbridled yearning…but would their castaway conditions lead to everlasting love?

#1619 BETWEEN STRANGERS—Linda Conrad
Lance White-Eagle was on his way to propose to another woman when he came across Marcy Griffin stranded on the side of the road. Circumstances forced them together during a horrible blizzard, and white-hot attraction kept their temperatures high. Could what began as an encounter between strangers turn into something so much more?

#1620 PRINCIPLES AND PLEASURES—Margaret Allison
CEO Meredith Cartwright had to keep playboy Josh Adams away from her soon-to-be-married sister. And what better way to do so than to throw herself directly into his path…and his bed. But Josh had an agenda of his own—and a deep desire to teach Meredith a lesson in principles…and pleasures!

SDCNM1004